There he was, in the corner of the room, his gaze fixed on her again.

In that instant, the other people in the room seemed to vanish. Or maybe they had turned into shadows, because the man in the corner was the only distinct thing she could see. She fought for breath—fought for sanity, if she was honest about it.

She thought of crossing the room and...touching him. That idea leaped into her mind, and she wondered where it had come from. Touch a stranger? Why?

Yet the compulsion was so strong that she started toward him.

She knew that at any moment he would come striding toward her. He would reach out and put his hand on her arm, and then what?

Everything would change.

BRIDAL JEOPARDY

USA TODAY Bestselling Author

REBECCA YORK

(Ruth Glick writing as Rebecca York)

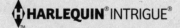
HARLEQUIN® INTRIGUE®

Norman, who's always there for me

Recycling programs
for this product may
not exist in your area.

ISBN-13: 978-0-373-69751-9

BRIDAL JEOPARDY

Copyright © 2014 by Ruth Glick

Printed in U.S.A.

ABOUT THE AUTHOR

Award-winning, *USA TODAY* bestselling novelist Ruth Glick, who writes as Rebecca York, is the author of more than one hundred books, including her popular 43 Light Street series for the Harlequin Intrigue line. Ruth says she has the best job in the world. Not only does she get paid for telling stories, she's also an author of twelve cookbooks. Ruth and her husband, Norman, travel frequently, researching locales for her novels and searching out new dishes for her cookbooks.

Books by Rebecca York

HARLEQUIN INTRIGUE

*43 Light Street
**Mindbenders

CAST OF CHARACTERS

Stephanie Swift—Was she marrying the wrong man?

Craig Branson—Why was he hiding his real identity?

John Reynard—Did he love Stephanie, or did he have other motives for marrying her?

Buck Arnot and Wayne Channing—Why were they hired to kidnap Stephanie?

Harold Goddard—What was his interest in Stephanie and Craig?

Henri Swift—Why was he desperate to have his daughter marry John Reynard?

Sam Branson—How did his murder change his brother's life?

Ike Broussard—Was the New Orleans cop helping or hindering Craig?

Claire Dupree—Where did Stephanie's assistant place her loyalties?

Prologue

The horror of that day had replayed over and over in Craig Branson's mind. What if he, Mom, Dad and Sam had gone to a different restaurant? What if they'd stayed home and ordered in? Life as he knew it would have continued on the same happy track.

But Dad had just brought in a big ad buy at the local TV station where he was promotions manager, and he'd been in the mood to celebrate his hard work.

"Where should we go to dinner?" he'd asked his twin sons, two dark-haired, dark-eyed boys only a few people could tell apart.

Craig and Sam were identical twins, born when a single egg had split in their mother's womb. Twins were supposed to be close, but there was more between these two eight-year-olds than anyone else knew. There was a hidden bond and a fierce love born of the connection they could never explain to anyone else.

They'd looked at each other and begun a silent conversation about the merits of various choices.

Then Sam had spoken for the two of them. He'd asked to go to Venario's, an Italian restaurant. If they ate at Venario's, they could order an extra pizza and have it for breakfast the next morning.

Mom had protested that pizza was no kind of breakfast,

but Dad let the boys have their way. If it made his twins happy to bring home pizza, he was all for it, as long as they had a nice portion of chicken or veal for dinner.

That evening they'd sat across from each other at the square table topped by a snowy cloth, silently debating the merits of ground beef or ham on their take-home pizza. Almost as soon as they'd come home from the hospital, they'd been able to read each other's thoughts, a skill they instinctively kept hidden from the world. Mom suspected, but she had never asked them about it because the idea was too outlandish for her to wrap her brain around. She was a down-to-earth woman who wanted her sons to be strong and independent, even when their inclination was to present a united front.

At the next table, a group of men was talking loudly; their voices annoyed Mom and Dad, but they didn't interfere with the Branson boys' happy conversation.

That was another what-if that had tortured Craig for the twenty-two years since that night when his whole world had been shattered.

What if he and Sam hadn't been so focused on each other? What if they'd been paying more attention to their surroundings?

Could Craig have saved Sam's life?

He didn't know because it all had happened so fast.

The door burst open, and two men had charged into the restaurant with guns drawn, already shooting as they ran. The guys at the next table hardly had time to react. One of them tried to stand and went down in a hail of bullets. Another one collapsed in his chair. And the third fell to the side, hitting Mom as she screamed in horror.

People all over the confined space were crying out and hitting the floor. But the chaos around Craig had hardly registered. His total attention was focused on Sam, who had been sitting closer to the scene of disaster.

He'd made a strangled sound and had fallen forward, his head hitting the table as blood spread across the crisp white cloth. His chest had been a mass of pain that Craig felt as though it were his own body on fire.

He'd leaped out of his seat, charging around the table to his brother's side, slipping from his father's grasp as he reached for Sam, struggling to maintain the fading connection between them. Panic rose inside him, and he'd clutched at his brother with his hand and with his mind.

Sam, don't leave me.

Craig?

Sam. I can't hear you, Sam.

I...can't...

Those were his last memories of his brother. He had started screaming then, his cries drowning out the sound of a siren approaching.

His father's arms had folded him close, protecting him from harm. But the harm was already done.

Sam was gone, vanished as though he had never been— leaving an aching gap in Craig's soul.

Despair and anger raged inside the boy who lived. But even at the age of eight, Craig knew that he would find out who had killed his brother and avenge his death.

Chapter One

The light from the computer screen gave a harsh cast to Craig Branson's angular features, yet he couldn't conceal the feeling of elation surging inside himself.

He'd only been eight when his twin brother had been cruelly ripped away from him, but on that terrible day, he'd vowed that he would find the killers and bring them to justice. Now, finally, he had a lead on one of the shooters in a gangland assassination twenty-two years ago.

The restaurant where crime boss Jackie Montana and two of his men had been gunned down had been full of witnesses. Many of the patrons had identified the killers from their mug shots. They were two hired hit men named Joe Lipton and Arthur Polaski who had taken jobs all over the U.S.

Although the cops knew the assassins' names, the men fled the scene and disappeared from the face of the earth. Now Craig knew why.

Unable to sit still, he stood and strode out of his office, then paced into the hall of the brick ranch house where he'd lived in Bethesda, Maryland, for the past few years.

It was in an upscale neighborhood just outside the nation's capital, the perfect place for the career he'd started planning even before Sam's funeral. He would make sure he was tough enough, smart enough and well trained enough to find his brother's killers. To that end he'd graduated from college at George Washington University, then enlisted in the army and gone to officer-candidate school right after basic training. From there he got his first choice of assignments, the military intelligence service. After learning everything he could about investigative techniques, he returned to civilian life and started his own detective agency.

When his dad died nine months after Mom, he inherited all the money he'd ever need—if you considered his unassuming lifestyle. He had no family. No wife and children, because he knew he was lacking something that most people took for granted—the ability to connect with others on a deep, personal level. He craved those things with a fierce sense of loss because he'd had them with Sam. When his brother had been ripped from him, his anchor to the human race had been severed.

Although that was a pretty dramatic way to put it, he understood the concept perfectly. Other people formed close friendships and loving relationships. He'd never been able to manage either, although he thought he faked it pretty well. He had friends. He'd had physically satisfying affairs with women, but he had always known that marrying one of them would mean cheating her out of the warmth and closeness she deserved.

Failing that, he'd focused on his work, partly because it was intensely rewarding to put bad guys away and partly because it was a means to an end.

He *would* find who had killed his brother, and he *would* make sure they would pay for what they had done.

He'd traveled around the U.S., and he maintained contacts with police departments all over the country. One of those contacts had just paid off big-time.

He walked back to his desk, activated the printer and

made a copy of the report that had come in from a lieutenant named Ike Broussard in the New Orleans P.D. According to the detective, the body of one of the men who had shot up that restaurant, Arthur Polaski, had just turned up dead on private property outside the city. The local police had identified him by dental records, and the murder weapon was with him.

A very neat package. Maybe too neat.

Craig skimmed the report again. Polaski was beyond his reach, but that didn't mean there would be no justice for Sam. The hit man hadn't been operating on his own. Every indication was that he'd been working for a local New Orleans bigwig named John Reynard.

As a boy, Craig had focused on bringing Polaski and Lipton to justice. But as he'd matured, he'd come to understand that the shooters were just hired thugs working for someone who wanted a rival crime boss dead. Now Polaski had led Craig to John Reynard.

Craig worked into the evening, collecting information on his quarry. Finally, when he saw that it was almost ten, he got up and stretched, then fixed himself a ham-and-cheese sandwich, which he took back to the computer, along with a bottle of beer. One advantage of living alone was that he didn't have to stick to regular meal times, eat at the table or stop work while he fueled up. Once he knew about Reynard, it was easy to find a boatload of information on the man. He was in his early sixties and owned an import-export business in New Orleans, probably a front for drug smuggling. But the cops apparently didn't look into his company too carefully, undoubtedly because Reynard was very generous with his bribes and also contributed significant amounts to local charities. Public record presented him as an upstanding citizen, although it was interesting that two of his former wives had died while married to him.

Craig took a swallow of beer as he came to an intriguing piece of information. Reynard was about to tie the knot again. In the society pages of the *Times-Picayune,* there were pictures of him with his bride-to-be at several charity events. She was a very lovely blonde woman named Stephanie Swift who looked to be half the age of the man she was going to marry.

Craig shook his head. He could see why Reynard was attracted to the woman. But what did she see in him?

As Craig studied her wide-set eyes, her narrow nose, her nicely shaped lips and the blond hair that fell in waves to her shoulders, he felt an unexpected jolt of awareness. Something about her drew him, and he struggled to dismiss the feeling of attraction to her. He didn't want to like her. What kind of a woman would marry a lowlife like Reynard? Could it be that she was too stupid or unaware to understand what kind of man her fiancé was? Or maybe she was attracted to his money, and she didn't care what the man was really like.

He made a snorting sound, then warned himself to stay objective. That usually wasn't a problem for him, but apparently it was with Ms. Swift, and letting himself feel anything for her would be a big mistake.

With another shake of his head, he clicked away from a smiling picture of her with Reynard and went back to her dossier. Apparently she came from a family that had been prominent in the city. But the Swifts must have fallen on hard times because now she spent her days in the dress shop that she owned in the French Quarter.

Well, she'd be able to give up that business and get back to her society lifestyle once she married Reynard.

But maybe in the meantime she'd be useful to Craig. What if he got to know her before he made a move on Reynard? Yes, that might be the way to go.

THE BELL OVER the shop door jingled, and Stephanie Swift looked up. It was a delivery man, carrying a long cardboard box. When she saw the logo on the package, she stiffened, but she kept her voice pleasant as she spoke to the deliveryman.

"Thanks so much."

He nodded to her as he set the package down on the counter and left her Royal Street shop.

Before the bell stopped jingling again, her assistant, Claire Dupree, came out of the back room, where she'd been unpacking merchandise that had arrived from New York that morning. Claire was a pretty, dark-haired young woman who wanted to get into fashion, and she'd offered to work for Stephanie at minimum wage for the chance to learn the business. She was a quick study, and Stephanie had come to rely on her.

"You've been expecting your wedding dress. Is that it?" she asked.

"Yes."

Claire eyed the box. "I'm dying to see it."

"We'll open it in the back room," Stephanie answered, struggling to sound enthusiastic. She'd known all along that John Reynard was the wrong man for her. Or she'd known that perhaps there *was* no right man, given the way she failed to connect with anyone on a truly intimate level. But she'd held out hope for…something more.

Then fate had overtaken her hopes.

Still, she wasn't going to let on to her assistant that she had doubts about her upcoming wedding. She was too private a person to talk about her secret worries. And she couldn't shake the nagging impression that it might be dangerous to reveal her state of mind to anyone. Besides, even if she weren't marrying John Reynard out of love, maybe it would turn out okay.

That was what she told herself, even when she feared she was heading for disaster. Too bad she was stuck with the bargain she'd made.

"Should I open the box?" Claire called from the next room.

"I'll be right there," she answered, then took a couple of deep breaths as she looked around the shop that had been the major focus of her life for the past two years. It was feminine and nicely decorated, a showplace where women could relax while they browsed the dresses and evening outfits that Stephanie imported from designers on the East Coast and Europe.

She'd always dressed well and loved fashion, but her interest morphed from an avocation into a business when her father had given her the bad news about his gambling debts.

She'd wanted to scream at him, but she hadn't bothered raging about his lack of regard for anyone but himself. The criticism would just roll off his back like rain off a yellow slicker.

Instead, she'd taken her sense of style and the money that her mother had left her and bought a small shop in the French Quarter, a shop that had done well until a downturn in the city's business cycle had put her in jeopardy.

She stepped into the back room and found Claire talking on her cell phone. When she saw Stephanie, she clicked off at once.

"Sorry. I was just checking in with Mom."

"Sure," Stephanie answered, distracted. She knew that Claire's mother was living in a nursing home and that her daughter spoke to her frequently.

Taking a pair of scissors, she began to carefully open the dress box. The top came off, revealing layers of tissue paper. Beneath them was an ivory-colored sleeveless gown decorated with seed pearls and delicate lace. She'd seen it at a wedding outlet in New York and had used her professional capacity to order it at the wholesale price.

"Beautiful," Claire breathed as she touched the delicate silk fabric.

"Yes."

"Why don't you try it on? I can help you with the buttons up the back."

"Not now."

Stephanie slipped the dress onto a hanger, then turned away to put it on the rack in back of her, where it dangled like a headless hanging victim.

She winced, wishing she hadn't thought of that image.

Of course, that wasn't the only thing she wished. What if she'd never met John Reynard? What if her shop hadn't taken that downturn? What if she met a man who could connect with her in ways that she could only imagine?

She made a disgusted sound. As if that was going to happen.

"What?" Claire asked.

"Nothing. I'm not really feeling well. Do you mind if I get out of here for a few hours?"

Claire gave her a sympathetic look. "Oh, no. You've got that reception with John this evening."

Stephanie felt a wave of anxiety sweep over her. She'd put the reception out of her mind, but now she knew what had been making her feel unsettled—even before the dress had arrived. "Lord, I forgot all about that."

"You'd better go home and rest. You don't want to disappoint him."

"Right." Once again, she wished that she'd never met John Reynard. Wished that he hadn't listened to her dad's sob story, then stepped in to pay her debts—and Dad's. But she'd taken his money because her father had begged her to let John Reynard handle their problems. And at the time, it had seemed the only way out. She'd been willing to let her shop go under. She could always find a job with someone else, but that wouldn't work out so well for Dad. He'd lose the house—his last tie to the luxurious past that the family had enjoyed. And she'd known deep down that would kill him.

If she were the cause of that, her guilt would be too great for her to bear. Which was the irony of this situation. She'd never really felt close to her parents, yet she was compelled to make sure her father ended his days in the manner to which he was accustomed. Probably because she'd never felt like a dutiful daughter—and Dad had made sure she understood that.

Claire's voice broke into her troubled thoughts.

"Don't worry about a thing. I'll take care of it."

"Thanks." She thought for a moment. "If Mrs. Arlington calls to ask about her ball gown, tell her it hasn't come in yet."

"Of course. Don't trouble yourself about it," Claire repeated.

Stephanie nodded, wishing she could really relax and stop worrying about her future.

Chapter Two

After three days in New Orleans, Craig was getting a feel
for the city and the power base that ran it. The Big Easy
was so different from any other American urban area that
it might as well have been in a foreign country. The atmo-
sphere was hot and sultry. The houses were painted bright
colors. The landscape was almost tropical, and the people
exuded a laid-back attitude that belied the hard times that
Hurricane Katrina had caused.

He'd avoided his contact with the police department because he was in the city under an assumed name—Craig
Brady. Unlike Craig Branson, Brady had inherited consid-
erable wealth and lived off his investments. The persona
was one he'd established several years ago when he'd been
hired to take down a finance guy who was using a Ponzi
scheme to line his own pockets. Craig had posed as an in-
vestor ripe for the picking and nailed the guy.

The Brady persona made a good cover for investigating
John Reynard. But so far Craig had stayed away from the
man. He wanted to establish himself as being in the city
for profit and fun. To that end he'd gone prowling around,
sampling the food, the jazz and the strip clubs along Bourbon Street.

He'd also found a high-stakes poker game at a private
gentleman's club, where he could pick up some money and

also some information. The minimum bet was fifty dollars, but that had been of little risk to Craig. He might not be good at intimate relationships, but he was excellent at reading people, and he used that skill to win a couple of sizable pots.

Then he'd allowed himself to lose half of it back, which put the men around the table in a friendlier mood than when he'd been raking in the chips.

"So where do you meet high-class women?" he'd asked as he and his new friends helped themselves to the club's bourbon.

"The United Hospital Fund is holding a charity event at Oak Lane Plantation, out along the river."

"Sounds interesting," he answered

"Tickets are a thousand clams a pop."

"Well, it's for a good cause," Craig allowed. "And you're saying that some of the ladies are single?"

"The young gals looking for husbands come out in droves."

He'd found out where to buy a ticket and purchased one, pretty sure from his research that John Reynard would be there.

After buying the ticket, he'd gone to one of the rental shops in town and gotten a tuxedo. Not his usual attire, he thought as he stood in front of the mirror, adjusting his bow tie. But he guessed he'd do.

His hand shook for a moment, and he pressed his palm against his thigh, annoyed at his unusual reaction. It came from being so close to Sam's killer, he told himself, but he wasn't entirely sure he believed it.

He couldn't contain the mixture of anticipation and nerves racing through him. He'd been waiting a long time to confront the man who had been responsible for his brother's death, and now the meeting was almost here.

Well, *confrontation* wasn't exactly the right word. He was going to have a look at John Reynard and start planning his attack on the man. After all these years, there was no rush. Reynard wasn't going anywhere. And neither was his beautiful fiancée. As Craig thought of Stephanie Swift, anticipation tightened his gut.

Stephanie Swift was not the main event, but she could be a means to an end, he told himself.

Craig walked to the parking lot and picked up his rental car, then headed out of town to Oak Lane Plantation.

The mansion house was ablaze with lights when he arrived, and he found a space among the Cadillacs, BMWs and Mercedes that dominated the parking area.

Inside he accepted a flute of champagne from a waiter hovering near the door because he didn't want to look out of place among the men and women enjoying themselves at this upscale gathering.

The mansion, which was often rented out for private functions, was lavishly furnished with period tables and chests interspersed with more modern chairs and sofas and Oriental rugs on the polished pine floorboards.

He wandered from the front hall to the other rooms on the main floor, watching the guests talking, drinking and eating. As promised, some of the ladies were young, and many gave him speculative looks, although he didn't stop to talk to any of them.

But he had his story ready if needed.

He was from out of town and considering settling in the city, and he thought this gathering would be an excellent introduction to the local social life. He'd act as if he was looking for new investments—and open to suggestions from the New Orleans financial elite.

He made his way slowly through the crowd and finally spotted John Reynard on the veranda. He was talking with a group of men and women who all seemed to know one another. And Stephanie Swift was at his side.

Craig had been taken with her picture. He hadn't been prepared for the reality of the woman. His breath caught as he looked at her from the doorway leading outside. She was stunning in an emerald-green gown that perfectly set off her blond beauty.

She must have known he was staring at her because she looked up, and he would have sworn she had the same reaction to him that he was having to her. Her breath hitched, and she went absolutely still.

Apparently Reynard sensed something. Bending close to her, he spoke in a low voice. From twenty feet away, Craig couldn't catch the words, but he understood the proprietary way the man spoke. This woman was his property.

She must have said something reassuring, because Reynard went back to his previous conversation. But the moment had been telling. From Stephanie's reaction, Craig knew that she understood her place in her fiancé's world.

He lingered in the doorway and took a small sip of his champagne, thinking that he'd like to approach the couple, but he wasn't going to press his luck. After a long moment, he turned away and went in search of the buffet table. He'd paid a lot of money to enjoy this reception, and he might as well get a decent meal out of it.

STEPHANIE WATCHED the broad shoulders of the man who had been staring at John—and her. She'd noticed him right away, noticed how his tuxedo accentuated his rugged good looks. She knew she had never seen him before. Who was he, and what was he doing here? For a moment he'd looked interested in John, then he'd switched his attention to her, and she'd felt as if there was an invisible wire connecting the two of them, drawing them to each other.

She hoped John hadn't caught the intensity of her interest in the man because she knew he was jealous of any interactions she had with other guys. John had staked his claim on her, and she fully understood that playing any role but the one she'd been assigned was dangerous. Before she'd agreed to the marriage, her suitor had done his best to charm her, and she'd tried to convince herself that marriage to him wouldn't be so bad. But once he'd known she was his, there had been subtle changes. He didn't outright say that he owned her, but she got that message.

"Excuse me for a moment," she murmured.

"Where are you going?" her companion asked.

"To powder my nose."

He nodded, and she moved back through the mansion toward the grand staircase. The ladies' room was on the second floor, and she was glad to escape from John and the society types who populated the party.

As she walked through the main floor, she scanned the crowd and was relieved and disappointed not to see the mysterious stranger. He couldn't have just come in for a few minutes and left. Not at the price he'd paid for the ticket to this event.

Then she felt the hairs on the back of her neck prickle and she turned quickly. There he was, in the corner, his gaze fixed on her again.

In that instant, the other people in the room seemed to vanish. Or maybe it was more accurate to say that they had turned into shadows, because the man in the corner was the only distinct thing she could see. She fought for breath, fought for sanity if she was honest about it.

What are you doing to me? she asked, the question never leaving her lips because she spoke only in her mind. Still, she had the weird feeling that he could hear her, although he gave her no answer.

She thought of crossing the room and…touching him. That idea leaped into her mind, and she wondered where it had come from. Touch a stranger? Why?

Yet the compulsion was so strong that she started toward him. Then she stopped after two steps and clenched her fists.

He was standing with the same rigidity, and she knew that at any moment he would come striding toward her. He would reach out and put his hand on her arm, and then what?

Everything would change.

She didn't know what that meant, and she didn't want to find out. No, that was a lie. She couldn't afford the luxury of finding out.

The temptation was so overwhelming that she had to force herself to turn away and hurry up the stairs. With a sigh of relief, she closed the ladies' room door behind her, putting a barrier between herself and the man who had drawn her like no other.

Marge LaFort glanced up from where she sat at one of the dressing-table stools. "Is something wrong?"

"No," she lied.

"You look like…"

"Like what?" she demanded as the other woman's voice trailed off.

Marge shrugged. "I'm not sure. Is that handsome fiancé of yours giving you a hard time?"

"No. Of course not," Stephanie denied. In fact, she had forgotten all about John Reynard when she'd been caught in the stranger's web. Or was he caught in hers? She didn't know which.

She walked through the dressing area and into the bathroom, where she used the facilities, not because she needed to but because it would seem strange to simply come here and take refuge.

To her relief, when she emerged, Marge was gone. Or was that good? What if Marge went straight down to talk to John?

Stephanie dragged in a breath and let it out, wishing that she didn't imagine every person in the mansion as a spy for John Reynard, yet she knew that he did have a network of informants—or at least people who were anxious to stay on the good side of such a powerful man by feeding him information about people and events he might think important.

For example, she knew there were some new customers who had come to her shop to check out John Reynard's fiancée. And some of them were probably reporting back to him, much as she hated to think it. But she supposed she'd have to live with that, and maybe he'd trust her more when they were married.

She stayed at the dressing table for several more minutes, fussing with her hair, wondering whom she was hiding from—the dark-haired man or her intended. When she finally emerged and came downstairs, she didn't see the stranger. That was a relief. Now she only had to deal with John.

MEN WERE WATCHING HIM, Craig realized as he filled a plate with boudin balls, Cajun rice and crawfish étouffée. Tough-looking types who didn't exactly fit in with the other guests at this fancy event. Since they were dividing their attention between Reynard and Craig, he had to assume that they were the other man's bodyguards. Apparently Craig had caught Reynard's attention. Or perhaps Reynard had noticed the silent exchange when Craig and Stephanie had made eye contact. At any event, he decided it would be best to leave.

After taking a few bites, he put down his plate on one of the trays set around the room for dirty dishes and made his way out of the house and into the parking area, half-expecting somebody to try to jump him. But apparently his leaving had the desired effect. He drove away and back to his upscale New Orleans B and B without incident.

But what was his next move?

He'd focused his research on John Reynard. Now he was going to find out everything he could about Stephanie Swift. He told himself he was doing his job. He told himself that digging into the woman's life would be the key to taking down Reynard, but he wasn't sure he was being honest about his motives. If he admitted he was obsessed with her, that would be more like the truth.

The feeling was a novelty for Craig. He'd enjoyed the company of women. He'd learned the art of pleasing them in bed. But none of them had drawn his interest the way Stephanie Swift had.

He had looked up details about her on the web, but that was too impersonal an approach. Switching his tactics, he decided to get a firsthand picture of her life.

The morning after the charity reception, he waited in his car outside her apartment on Decatur Street and discreetly followed her Honda sedan to a sprawling mansion in the Garden District. It was her father's house, he knew, and he drove around the corner and waited until she emerged about a half hour after she'd entered, a frown on her pretty features. Apparently her meeting with Dad hadn't gone so well.

Her next stop was her shop on Royal. When she went in, he walked past and took up a discreet position around the corner.

He thought of himself as good at surveillance, but he wondered if she knew he was following her. Not because a normal person would have caught on, but because there was something between them that he couldn't explain. He'd been prepared to dislike her. Instead, he'd been drawn to her when they'd seen each other at that charity reception, and she'd been as aware of him as he was of her.

That knowledge set up an unaccustomed buzzing inside him. He hadn't felt this way since…

Well, since he and Sam had played hide-and-seek. Only back then it had been a different kind of game. Most kids hid and hoped that the other person couldn't figure out where they had gone. With him and Sam, there was an extra element. One of them would hide, then try to break the connection between them—try to be as quiet as possible in his mind so that his brother would have no idea where he was.

Sam had been better at it than Craig, who hadn't been able to turn off his thoughts, and Sam had always found him. But why was he thinking of that *now?*

TWO DAYS AFTER the charity reception, Stephanie was still feeling unsettled as she went through the rack of clothing on the left side of the shop, buttoning blouses, straightening straps and generally making the merchandise look tidy. She struggled to stay calm, but her heart was pounding. She couldn't shake the feeling that something was going to happen, and every so often, she glanced toward the window, wondering if she was going to see the dark-haired man with the broad shoulders who had stared at her in the plantation house. Well, it hadn't been just him. She'd stared back because there had been something about him that had compelled her interest. It wasn't simply the way his formal attire had set off his dark good looks. She'd felt a pull toward him that she couldn't explain, even to herself. A pull that excited her and made her nerves jump at the same time.

The bell over the door jingled, and she went rigid. As she turned, she thought she would see the man from the reception. Instead, two rough-looking guys came striding in as though they owned the place.

Both of them were wearing light-colored business suits that seemed out of place on anyone so tough-looking. One was short and completely bald—or he'd shaved off any remaining hair on his head. He was trying for a Yul Brynner effect, although his face was too ugly for a movie star—unless he was playing a Mafia heavy. The other guy was a couple of inches taller, with a wide mouth, bushy eyebrows and thick, wavy hair.

They both had big hands and beady, assessing eyes. Or perhaps the better word was *hungry.*

Neither one of them would inspire confidence in a dark alley at night. But here they were in her shop, and she was pretty sure that neither one of them had come to buy a dress for his girlfriend.

"Nice place you have here," the taller one said.

As they stood looking her over, her mouth turned so dry that she could barely speak, but she managed to say, "Can I help you?"

The spokesman answered. "That depends, sweetheart."

"On what?"

"On what you have to offer."

"Nothing," she heard herself say.

"We'll see."

She took a step back, wishing that Claire wasn't out on her lunch break. But what good would Claire do against these guys?

Maybe call 911 from the back room, if she'd been here.

But Stephanie was on her own, and she was sure that they already knew it. Wishing the counter were between her and the men, she took a step to the side. One of them kept pace with her while the other one stood by the door. She saw him turn, and she had the awful feeling that he was planning to lock the three of them in there.

Chapter Three

Before the thug could accomplish his purpose, the door burst open, and another man charged into the shop. She had a split second to see who it was. The darkly handsome stranger from the charity reception. The other night, he'd been in a tuxedo. Today he had on jeans and a dark T-shirt.

The man in the doorway reacted to the interruption by reaching into his coat, perhaps for a gun, but he never connected with whatever he was going to pull out. The stranger cracked him in the jaw with a large fist, then pushed him backward into the other man. They both went down in a tangle of arms and legs, pulling some of the clothing from the rack with them, but it wasn't going to be that easy to get rid of them.

The one on the bottom threw his partner to the side and pulled an automatic from his pocket. Stephanie reacted instinctively. She kicked out with her high-heeled shoe, catching the guy in his gun hand, making him howl in pain. She followed the kick by stamping down on the back of his hand, drawing a scream and sending the gun flying.

The bald one had scrambled up and launched himself at the stranger, who was prepared for the move. He stepped aside, letting baldy crash into the glass of the door. He made a strangled sound as he bounced back, then reached for the knob and flung the door open. He was outside and running down the block before Stephanie realized that the other man was on his feet and trying to get away as the rescuer made a grab for him. But the thug had the strength of desperation. He pushed the stranger against the wall, then leaped around him, charging out the door, following his partner down the block.

The man who had come to Stephanie's rescue pushed himself upright, determination in his eyes, and she was afraid he was going after the two men. She grabbed his hand to stop him, and everything changed.

In that moment of contact, the breath whooshed from her lungs, and she stood staring at him—as she had stared when they'd been standing across the room from each other at the plantation house. Only this was different. Last time there had been twenty feet of space between them. Now her hand gripped his, and somehow the physical connection had opened a gateway between them.

Images flooded into her mind. She saw a long-ago scene. Two little boys in a restaurant. She knew one of them was… Craig. His name was Craig. And the other one was Sam. And their minds were open to each other the way his mind was open to her at this moment.

The other boy was his mirror image. He must be his twin brother. There was a completeness to the two of them, a bond that made her sharply aware of all the unfulfilled longings that permeated her life.

She was just sinking into the long-ago scene when the door of the restaurant where the boys were sitting flew open, and gunmen charged in—like the men who had charged into her shop. Only these guys had assault rifles, and they started shooting.

She felt the seconds of fear. She felt the pain as Sam was hit. She felt Craig's utter desolation as his brother slipped away from him.

Gasping, she tried to pull back, but his hold only tightened on her, and she knew he was pulling memories from her mind as she was from his.

More recent memories. The talk with her father where he'd told her that he couldn't pay off his gambling debts. And then the look in his eyes when he explained that there was a solution to all their problems. A rich man was interested in marrying her. A rich man who would take care of their debts and take care of her for the rest of her life.

"He spoke to you first?" she asked her father.

"Yes."

"Why?"

"He thought that was more appropriate."

Was that the real reason, or had he known that he had an advantage with the father that he didn't have with the daughter?

She found out her suitor was John Reynard, a man she had met at the country club out by Lake Pontchartrain, where she'd gone for a friend's birthday celebration. He was another guest at the party, and he'd sat at her table and talked to her. They'd danced, and she'd known he was interested in her. He'd asked her out several times, and she'd accepted because she saw no harm in it. But the idea of his wanting to marry her came as a shock.

"I'm not ready for marriage," she blurted.

"You're going to have to change your mind about that."

"No."

"I'm in financial trouble."

"Whose fault is that?"

"You could say it's my own fault, but I'm not going to go down in disgrace if someone is willing to help me. Besides, John Reynard will make a good husband. He's rich and well connected. You'll never want for anything."

She felt as though she were living in the Middle Ages.

Women in the twenty-first century married for love, not for the right connections.

Yet she'd long ago secretly given up on love, and maybe that was why she had finally agreed.

She didn't want to be revealing any of that to Craig Branson. Or was it Craig Brady? She couldn't be sure, because both names came to her strongly.

But the exchange of information was only part of what was happening between them. She felt his emotions. The emptiness that had consumed him since his brother's death. It was like the emptiness she had always felt, only she'd had nothing to compare it to.

And below the mental connection was a sexual pull that she had never experienced before in her life.

It was as though she must make love with this man—or die. Or perhaps she *would* die if she made love with him.

That thought was so outrageous that she pushed it from her thoughts. Which wasn't difficult, because sexual desire was limiting her ability to think.

Craig Branson or Brady pulled her into his arms and lowered his mouth to hers.

She wanted to push him away. No, that was a lie. She wanted him to show her the pleasure of making love—pleasure that she knew would never be hers with John Reynard.

She tried to drive that last thought from her mind as his lips moved over hers, hungry and insistent. It was too private to share with anyone, least of all the man who held her in his arms. But she knew he had picked it up and knew he was glad she understood what a mistake it would be to marry Reynard. Not just because…

Branson cut the thought off before it could fully form. She was sure that he and Reynard had never met each other before the night of the charity reception, yet he seemed to know a lot about her fiancé.

She tried to hang on to that observation, but her mind was no longer operating in any rational manner.

Feelings had become more important than thoughts. The feel of Craig Branson's lips against hers. The feel of his hands as they stroked up and down her back, then cupped her bottom, pulling her more tightly against the erection straining at the front of his jeans.

He was ready to make love with her. And she was just as ready, yet she knew in some part of her mind that this was going too fast. They had to stop, and she was the one who had to do it.

She wrenched her mouth away from his and pushed at his shoulders.

The move caught him by surprise, because in his mind he was already taking the heated contact to its logical conclusion.

She slipped out of his grasp and put several feet of space between them as she stood panting.

When he reached for her, she shook her head. "Not now."

He was breathing hard, and his face looked as if he'd just touched a live electric wire, but he said only, "Why not?"

Now she couldn't meet his heated gaze. "Is this usually the way you act with a woman you don't know?"

"You know it isn't."

"What happened between us just now?"

"I felt the connection to you. Like the connection to Sam." He laughed. "Well, I never felt the sexual part with my brother."

She nodded slowly.

"But you've never felt anything like that?" he asked.

"No. What does it mean?"

"You weren't a twin?"

"No."

"Then what in the hell just happened?" he asked, revealing he was as perplexed as she was.

"I don't know," she answered.

It seemed he was still trying to come to a logical conclusion when she was sure there was no logic to what had happened. Or, at least, no logic that she had ever encountered.

"I..."

Before she could explain that to him, the bell over the shop door jingled, and her head jerked up. Claire stepped into the shop and gave the two of them an appraising look.

"What's going on?" she asked, her voice going high and sharp.

"Two men came in here. I don't know what they wanted, except that they were going to hurt me. Then Mr...."

"Brady," he supplied, and she knew when he said it that it wasn't his real name. But for some reason he had decided to use it.

"Mr. Brady came in and fought with them. Then they ran away."

Claire's gaze swung to him, her eyes assessing. "That was lucky—your being here. But how did you know what was happening?"

"I was on my way to the po'boy shop down the block," the man who had rescued her said. "I noticed them on the street, and they looked out of place. When I saw them come in here, I didn't think they were planning to buy dresses."

Claire was still staring at Stephanie and Craig as though she didn't believe a word of what they saying. And Stephanie silently acknowledged that they were lying— by implication, at least, about what had happened after the men had left.

Craig turned away and came down on his knees under the rack of dresses. When he stood again, he was holding a gun. "They left this," he said to Claire.

She sucked in a sharp breath as she saw the weapon. If Claire hadn't believed them in the first place, she would now.

"What should I do with it?" Stephanie asked.

"I'll take it," Craig said.

"Shouldn't we call the police?"

"Do you want to?"

She thought about it before shaking her head, then wondered if he would accept the decision.

As she looked at him, her gaze zeroed in on the bruise that was discoloring his forehead.

"You got hurt in the fight," she said.

"Did I?"

"Yes. Your forehead is bruised. You need ice on that."

Glad to escape, she slipped into the back room, where she paused to run a shaky hand through her hair, thanking her lucky stars that she and Craig hadn't been in each other's arms when Claire had come in. That was all she needed, for someone to report back to John that she was kissing another man. Would Claire have ratted on her? She didn't know, but she still understood that she had to be careful.

She got several ice cubes from the refrigerator, wrapped them in a paper towel, then put them into a plastic bag. She wished she didn't have to go out there and face Craig again, but she was pretty sure he was still waiting for her in the front of the shop.

He and Claire were talking when she returned and handed him the ice pack, being careful not to touch his hand.

Something had happened between them when they touched, and she didn't want it to happen again. At least not now.

He took the ice and pressed the package against his forehead.

"Thanks."

"No problem."

"Mr. Brady and I were talking. He's in the city to get some investment advice," Claire said.

Stephanie nodded. She hadn't picked that up from him, but she supposed it could be true. She canceled the last silent observation. He wasn't in town for investment advice. He was here to investigate John Reynard.

That realization made her suck in a sharp breath.

"Are you all right?" Claire asked, her gaze anxious.

"I'm…I'm just reliving the moments before Mr. Brady came in," she answered. "It was pretty scary with those men coming after me."

"What happened, exactly?" Claire asked.

"Not too much. They came in, and I could tell they—" she gulped "—wanted to harm me."

"Why?" Claire pressed.

"I don't know," she answered, flapping her arm in frustration and wondering if it had something to do with her father. What if he'd let his gambling get out of hand again and they were here to make sure he paid up?

Nothing like that had happened to her before. Nobody had come after her because of her father's debts, but maybe she'd been lucky in the past.

Craig was also staring at her. Afraid he might try to touch her, she took a quick step back.

"Are you all right?" he asked.

"Yes."

"I'd better go."

She felt relief. She needed some distance from him. But the relief was tinged with disappointment. They had made some kind of weird mental connection, and she couldn't simply let that go. She wanted to ask if she would see him again, but she couldn't start a conversation like that in front of Claire. And she already knew the answer, because she understood that she and Craig Brady couldn't keep away from each other.

She shivered, drawing a reaction from Claire again.

"You should go home and rest."

"I can't keep bugging out on you."

"You've just had a pretty bad experience."

She might have argued except that she wanted to be alone with her thoughts—and her reactions.

OUTSIDE ON THE STREET, Craig took a deep breath, then looked around, making sure that the two men who had attacked Stephanie weren't lurking.

Perhaps if the other woman hadn't come in, Craig would have stayed in the shop. But their privacy had been compromised. Which was lucky, because following through on his impulses would have been dangerous for Stephanie.

He thought about her reaction to his question about calling the cops. A regular, upstanding citizen would have wanted to report the incident, but she'd decided not to do it. Which was good for him, he supposed. If he got dragged into making a police report, he'd have to give his real name.

He wasn't quite steady on his feet as he walked down the sidewalk, not sure where he was going.

His head was spinning as he tried to take in everything that had happened in the past hour. Starting with the attack and ending with the intimacy of his contact with Stephanie. He was still reeling from that. Probably she was, too, although he knew her reaction wasn't exactly the same as his.

From the contact with her, he knew that she had never experienced anything like what had happened when they'd touched. She'd been totally unprepared for the way their minds had connected.

To be honest, he hadn't been prepared, either. But it was

different for him. He had known that kind of mind-to-mind
contact before—with his brother. He'd mourned Sam's loss
and mourned the loss of that perfect communication. He'd
thought he would never experience it again. Then he had—
with Stephanie Swift. A woman who was engaged to marry
the man who had caused Sam's death.

He swore under his breath, trying to wrap his mind
around all the implications. If she married Reynard, she'd
be lost to him. And lost to herself, too, because she'd be
committing herself to a man who didn't understand her and
couldn't give her the intimate contact she needed.

Craig huffed out a breath. And he could?

Yes, of course. He'd proved it when he'd touched her,
kissed her. Their minds had opened to each other, but there
was an added component he'd never experienced with his
brother. He and Sam had been twin brothers, sharing the
intimacy of siblings. He and Stephanie were adults—and
intimate on a whole new level. Not only could they communicate mind to mind, they were drawn to each other with
a sexual pull that was startling in its intensity.

He wanted to make love with her. Desperately. Yet below
the surface of that need was a hint of warning. The sexual
contact was dangerous if they didn't handle it right. He
wasn't sure why he realized that truth. He only knew that
he wasn't making it up.

Something else he knew. He couldn't allow Stephanie
Swift to marry John Reynard for a whole lot of reasons. Yet
he knew that was another thing he'd have to handle carefully if he didn't want Stephanie to end up dead.

He winced. That was putting it pretty strongly, but he
couldn't discount that truth. John Reynard would fight for
what he thought was his. And if he couldn't have it, nobody could.

And what about Craig's original purpose—to avenge

his brother's death? He hadn't forgotten about that, but he knew he couldn't simply go blasting into Reynard's life. All along he'd known he had to be careful about his approach to the man. That was true in spades now.

Chapter Four

"You don't mind staying here by yourself?" Stephanie asked her assistant again.

"I think I'll be okay."

"I'd hate for anything to happen to you."

Claire gave her a direct look. "The way it sounded, they were after you—not me."

She answered with a tight nod.

"Go on, then." Claire looked around. "And maybe you want to take the back way."

Stephanie hated the idea of sneaking out of her own shop, but she knew that Claire was probably right. She slipped through the back door and stood looking around before heading down the alley and over a few blocks to the house she'd bought. She kept herself from running, but she walked quickly along the afternoon streets. When she stepped inside her living room, she breathed a sigh before locking the door firmly behind her, then looking around at the room she had so lovingly furnished—with some pieces from the Garden District mansion and others that she'd picked up at flea markets and garage sales.

The house itself was old but charming, and she'd gotten it at a very good price after Katrina, from a couple who had decided to leave the city for a safer environment.

The down payment had taken a chunk of the money she'd inherited from her mother. But she hadn't wanted to live with her father in the Garden District mansion. She'd been happy here—well, as happy as she could be. And now her life had turned itself upside down *again*.

The first time had been a few months ago, when John Reynard had asked for her hand in marriage, and she'd known she had to accept. Then an hour ago, Craig Branson had touched her, and the world had flipped over again.

Her mind had opened to Craig's. And his to hers. He'd tried to hide it from her, but she knew he had come to New Orleans because he thought John Reynard had something to do with the death of his twin brother. That was why he'd been at the charity reception the other night. He'd been stalking Reynard—and he'd locked eyes with her.

She thought about that and about what else she'd discovered. Since birth and perhaps before, Craig had been tied to his brother, Sam, in a way that he had taken for granted. That connection had been ripped away by a stray bullet, leaving him hardly able to cope with his life. But he had coped. And he'd vowed to avenge his brother's death.

She shuddered as she thought about the rest of what had been in his mind. He'd never expected to experience that intimacy with anyone again—but he had. With her.

What did it mean? How was it possible?

She was trying to work her way through the encounter with him when a knock on the door made her whole body jerk.

Was that Craig? Coming after her.

"Who's there?" she called out.

"John."

Oh, Lord, John. The man she was going to marry. One of the last people she wanted to see now.

She got up on shaky legs and crossed to the door. From the front window, she saw John standing on her doorstep, his arms folded tightly across his chest. He dropped them to his sides when he saw her staring at him.

Quickly she unlocked the door and stepped aside. He came in and closed the door behind him, then turned to her.

"What are you doing here?" she asked.

"You were attacked."

"How do you know?"

He hesitated for just a second before saying, "I was calling to say hello, and Claire answered the phone. She sounded upset, so I asked her some questions. Are you all right?"

"Yes."

"She says two men came into the shop and threatened you. Then a stranger came to your rescue."

"Yes."

"I assume you got his name."

"He's Craig Brady," she said, using the false name that he'd given to Claire.

"And you never met him before?"

She wondered what the right answer was, then decided and said, "I didn't meet him, but he was at that charity reception the other night."

"The guy who was watching you?"

She winced. "I guess. I didn't really pay much attention," she lied.

John kept his gaze on her, and she worked to keep her expression neutral. She knew he'd noticed Craig at the plantation house. And done what? Maybe had his guys make a move on him?

"So what about the men who attacked you?" John asked. "Had you ever seen *them* before?"

"No."

John continued his interrogation. "And what did they want?"

"I never found out."

His eyes narrowed. "But I suspect you think it has something to do with your father."

Her mouth had gone dry, but she managed to answer, "Yes."

"He's gambling again?"

"I...don't know for sure."

"You'd better tell him to behave himself. I'm not a bottomless well of money."

"I understand."

"I hate it that he's responsible for bad stuff happening to you," he said, the tone of his voice changing. She knew that change. He was feeling tender toward her, and amorous.

He reached out and took her in his arms, cradling her against himself, and she fought to keep the stiffness out of her body. She didn't want him to hold her, but she could hardly object to her fiancé comforting her after a frightening experience.

He crooked one hand under her chin and tipped her face up as he lowered his mouth. His lips touched down on hers, settled, then began to move with the skill of a man who had made love to many women.

Stephanie tried to relax and kiss him back, when all she wanted to do was duck out of his arms and flee the room.

He was an experienced lover, and she'd convinced herself that marrying him wouldn't be a personal disaster for her, yet, as he kissed her, she couldn't stop herself from comparing her feelings now to the sensations and emotions that had threatened to swamp her when Craig had held her in his arms.

Then she'd been aroused. Hot and pliable and ready for sex. Now she was only tolerating the attentions of the man whose bed she would share in a few months.

She hoped he didn't realize what she was really feeling. And when he drew back, she felt relief and shame warring inside her. If she were honest, she would tell John Reynard that she couldn't marry him, but she knew that was as impossible as her flying off to Oz in a hot-air balloon.

At least he hadn't forced her to make love with him. She'd told him that she couldn't do that until they were married, and he'd grumbled about the edict. But he'd respected her wishes. She wondered if he thought she was a virgin. Probably not. Probably he'd investigated her background enough to know that she'd been intimate with a few men, but the relationships had never gone very far. Maybe he was thinking that he'd wait until marriage so she didn't have a chance to walk away when she was disappointed.

He looked down at her. "I guess you're still upset by what happened."

"Yes. I'm sorry."

"I should let you rest." The edge in his voice made her grasp his arm. "I'm sorry. I just can't…" She let her voice trail off rather than try to explain any further.

"I'm going to have some of my men protect you," he said.

Her gaze shot to his face. "What do you mean?"

"They'll be watching over you."

"You mean they're coming here?"

"They won't bother you, but they'll be around."

"Yes, thank you," she managed to say, when she really wanted to scream at him to leave her alone.

He left the house then, and she collapsed into a chair, glad to be alone. Yet at the same time she was terrified by what had just happened. She'd never wanted to marry this man. Now she understood just how bad a decision it would be.

Would be? Was she still thinking that she had a choice?

FOR THE PAST FEW DAYS, Craig had been following Stephanie around. Now it was more important than ever for him to keep up the surveillance—not just for himself but for her. But as he rounded the corner at the end of her block, he saw John Reynard leaving her house.

He stopped short, ducking back around the corner, fighting a spurt of jealousy that stabbed through him. That bastard had access to Stephanie, and Craig did not. She was engaged to the man, but she was never going to marry him. Craig would make sure of that. The depth of his emotions shocked him. He hadn't felt this strongly about *anything* since Sam's death. Then he'd been filled with despair. But also determination, he acknowledged.

The determination was just as strong now, along with an excitement that coursed through his veins and made his heart pound.

He had to pry Stephanie away from John Reynard, but he couldn't exactly pull out a gun and shoot the man. He had to get something on him—something that would stop him in his tracks. Evidence from Sam's murder? He'd been prepared to play a long game getting that kind of information. But now the time frame had changed. It would be much better if it was something more recent that they could take to the cops.

They? Was he already thinking Stephanie was on his side?

He pulled himself up short. *Take it a step at a time,* he warned himself. *You just met her. You can't change her world in a couple of hours.*

Still, he did feel a small measure of victory. Reynard had

come running over to Stephanie's house after the incident. Probably he'd thought he could comfort her—like in the bedroom. But now he was on his way out the front door. Hopefully because Stephanie hadn't wanted him there.

How could she, after the connection she and Craig had made in the shop?

John left the house, but before he drove away, he glanced toward two men sitting in a car across the street from her house.

The men who had attacked her in the shop?

What would it mean that Reynard knew they were here?

Craig waited with his heart pounding until Reynard had finished his conversation with Stephanie and driven away. He ached to stride down the block and confront the watchers, but caution made him walk back in the other direction, then take the alley in back of the houses across the street from Stephanie's. They were typical French Quarter dwellings, many of them built butting up against one another or with enclosed courtyards, but there were passageways between some, and he took one that would bring him almost up to the car where the men were sitting.

He stayed in the shadows, noting that they were both turned toward Stephanie's house. He recognized them. They weren't the thugs who had come into her shop. They were the men who had followed him around at the charity reception. John Reynard's bodyguards. Apparently, after the disturbing incident in the shop, he'd assigned them to watch over his fiancée.

In a way, that was a good move on Reynard's part. And it argued that Reynard had nothing to do with the attack at the dress shop, but it created a problem for Craig. He needed to get close to her again, and he'd have to make sure the men didn't spot him. For a couple of reasons—chief of which was that it would put Stephanie at risk.

He cursed under his breath, feeling as if Reynard was beating him in a chess game. Craig was going to have to rethink his strategy.

STEPHANIE STOOD, too restless to simply sit and do nothing. Instead she went to the window and lifted one of the venetian-blind slats. She spotted the men in the car across the street immediately. As promised, they were keeping watch on her house. But she saw something else, as well. A flicker of movement drew her attention to a passageway between two houses near the bodyguards' car. A man was standing in the shadows, watching the watchers. For a moment she thought it might be one of the men who had come to the shop. But that was only until she saw his face.

It was Craig Branson. He must have followed her home, and now he was watching the two men in the car.

Were there more of John's men guarding the rear of her house? She'd have to assume that was true, since she could leave that way and not be spotted from the street.

Feeling like a prisoner in her own home, she gritted her teeth. But maybe that was the way John wanted her to feel. He'd said he'd arranged protection, but knowing him, that probably wasn't his only reason. He wanted her to understand that if she stepped out of line, he would know it.

She let the slat slip back into place, glad that the men out there couldn't see through the walls of her house. Crossing to the kitchen, she got out a box of English breakfast tea. After filling a mug with water, she set it in the microwave and pressed the beverage button.

When the water was hot, she added a tea bag and let it steep while she paced back and forth along the length of the kitchen, waiting for the tea to be ready. After removing the tea bag, she carried the mug to the office, where she sat down at the computer and thought back over the details of her encounter with Craig Branson. From the mind-to-mind contact, she knew a lot about him already. Or maybe none of that was true.

She made a dismissive sound. How would it be possible to lie when you communicated mind to mind with someone? Maybe if you rehearsed a story and fixed it firmly in your thoughts. But if you weren't expecting the contact, you'd be taken by surprise. That had been true of her and true of Branson, as well. But there was one more possibility she had to consider. What if he was a lunatic who believed the story he'd given her?

She clenched her fists so hard that her nails dug into her palms. Deliberately, she relaxed. The encounter had knocked her off-kilter, but if she was trying to say he was insane, she was grasping at straws, probably because she didn't want to deal with the shock of what happened when they'd touched each other.

That observation gave her pause. She'd been alone all her life, and wasn't this what she'd been longing for—a soul mate?

But just at the wrong time. She had already committed herself to another man—a man who considered her his property. What could she hope for with Craig Branson? Was this going to be like that old movie, *The Graduate,* where the guy comes charging down from San Francisco to stop the woman he loves from marrying the wrong guy? He's too late to prevent the ceremony, but he takes the bride away anyway.

Was that the fantasy she was hoping for?

Unable to cope with her own muddled thoughts, she put the name Craig Branson into Google and got several hits. There was more than one man by that name, but she quickly zeroed in on the right one.

He owned a private security company, which meant he

thought he could go up against John Reynard. But he didn't know Reynard.

She'd assumed she knew the man, but she was becoming more and more shocked by the things she found out. Not dark facts, but his attitude of owning her—and having her father enslaved to his will.

With a shudder, she put Reynard out of her mind and went back to the information on Craig Branson.

Searching back, she found a newspaper article that made her chest go tight. It was an account of the incident that had killed Craig's brother. There was a picture of a smiling little boy, obviously a school portrait. He was what she'd imagine Craig would have looked like at the age of eight.

So it was true. He hadn't made up the story. Her heart was pounding as she scanned the text, reading about the murder of a mob boss in a restaurant and how some of the innocent diners had gotten shot. Most had been wounded. The only fatality was Sam Branson.

The article told her something else. The target in the restaurant had been a mob boss. If John Reynard had something to do with his death, what did that make him? She pushed that question out of her mind because it was more than she could cope with. Which left her contemplating the tragedy.

She sat for a moment, imagining Craig's reaction to the loss of his brother—and imagining what it must have been like for him to touch her and get back that kind of closeness. Lord, what would her life have been like if she'd had a brother or a sister she could communicate with that way? And what if she'd lost them?

But she'd never had a brother or a sister. She'd once heard her parents talking in whispers about her mom having trouble getting pregnant. She'd gathered that they'd gone to a fertility clinic, but she'd never directly asked about it, because it had seemed like something they wanted to keep quiet.

As she thought about it, long-ago memories came back to her. She remembered being in a waiting room with a lot of other children. Could that have had something to do with the clinic?

It didn't seem likely because she hadn't been a baby. Maybe she'd had some illness and her parents had taken her to a specialist?

She wasn't sure, and probably it wasn't important. Or maybe it was. She was getting married. Would she have trouble getting pregnant?

A shudder went through her. She wanted children. Maybe she could be close to her own children, the way she'd never been close to her parents. But did she want to have children with John Reynard?

The idea sent another frisson through her. She'd felt trapped the moment she'd agreed to the marriage with Reynard, but meeting Craig Branson had made it worse. Unfortunately, she was drawn to him as she'd never been to her fiancé.

She closed her eyes, willing those thoughts out of her mind. Thoughts of Reynard and of Branson. She had a more immediate problem. Men had come to her shop and threatened her, and she'd better talk to her father about it.

She turned off her computer and looked out the window, seeing the men in the car across the street. They were supposed to be protecting her, but her impulse was to slip away without their knowing it. Because she didn't trust John? Or because she didn't like the idea of his having her followed? And she had the feeling that would only get worse if they married.

Chapter Five

Instead of walking out the front door, Stephanie slipped into the courtyard at the side of her house. From there, she went into the alley where her car was parked. Before she'd gotten two blocks from home, she looked in the rearview mirror and saw that she was being followed—by the men who had been sitting out front.

How did they even know she'd left the house? Apparently there was some mechanism for spying on her that she didn't know about and didn't understand.

As she drove to her father's Garden District mansion, she kept glancing in the rearview mirror, checking the men behind her who were making no attempt to hide the fact that they were following. She drove around the block, partly to make the men wonder what she was doing and partly to have a look at the house. Once it had been painted in shades of cream, purple and green to create the classic "painted lady" effect that was so popular in the Garden District, with different colors used to accent different parts of the trim. But the paint had faded, making the house look sad instead of distinctive.

And the shrubbery was overgrown, contributing to the general air of neglect. She hadn't really looked at the exterior in ages, and it was a shock to see how much the property had gone downhill in the past few years.

When she finally pulled into the driveway, the men stopped on the street in front of the house, watching her through the screen of shrubbery as she walked to the wide front porch. She knocked to let her father know that she was there, then used her key to let herself in.

Once again, she stopped to notice details that she hadn't paid much attention to in years because they were simply part of the environment. Now she looked around at the familiar furnishings, many of which had been handed down through several generations.

The front hall boasted a long, antique marble-topped chest, centered under an elaborate gilded mirror. Both of them needed dusting. And in the sitting room to her right, she saw the old sofas and chairs that had been in the house since before she was born.

"Dad?"

"Out here," he called.

She walked through the kitchen that hadn't been updated since the seventies and into the sunroom that spanned the back of the house. It had always been her favorite room, filled with blooming plants and wrought iron and wicker furniture. And she noted that her father must be keeping it up because the plants all looked healthy.

He was in his favorite wicker chair, where he could look into the room or out at the formal garden. Although the plants in the sunroom were well tended, the back garden was more bedraggled than the front. When she was little, they'd had a crew come by several times a week. Now it was probably once a month, and the neglect showed. Really, she should come over here to trim some of the bushes.

In her spare time, she thought. She was plenty busy with her shop and with the wedding preparations.

She had given the house and garden a critical inspection. Now she did the same thing with her father, who was in his early seventies. Once he'd been a vigorous man. Now his broad shoulders were stooped, and his white hair was thinning on top. His complexion had always been ruddy. The color hadn't faded, but the lines in his face were more prominent.

He was dressed in a crisp white shirt, a blue-and-red-striped tie, a navy sports jacket and gray slacks as though he might be ready to receive company. The sartorial statement was a holdover from the old days. The world might have switched to casual dress, but her father had stayed with his traditions.

He looked up to meet her gaze.

"You were just here a couple of days ago. Now what?"

It wasn't a very warm welcome. No "Hello" or "How are you?" But she was used to that kind of reaction from him. She and her father had never had that great a relationship, and it had deteriorated after her mother had died five years ago of ovarian cancer. It had been a quick death because her mother had kept her symptoms to herself until it was too late to do anything about the cancer.

When Stephanie had been a kid, Mom had tried to keep up the appearance of a warm, close family, and maybe she fooled some people who didn't know them all that well. Dad had always done his own thing. He'd had a sales job that had taken him out of town frequently. Being away from his family had given him the opportunity to gamble. He'd retired several years ago, but since his wife's death, there had been no one to pull him back from his gambling obsession. Which was how he'd gotten into debt and almost lost the house—until John Reynard had approached him about marrying his daughter.

Dad had always been a pretty decent poker player. In fact, there were many times when he'd won instead of lost. In her more cynical moments, Stephanie wondered if John had somehow arranged for her father to lose—so he could approach him with the offer of financial salvation.

"You know I like to stop by and see how you're doing," she answered.

"I'm doing fine," he said, his brittle voice a counterpoint to the claim.

"That's good."

"What's bothering you?" he asked bluntly.

She might have taken the time to work up to her question, but since he was forcing the issue, she asked, "Are you gambling again?"

He sat up straighter in his chair when he answered, "I agreed not to."

"That wasn't the question," she said, determined to meet his words with equal force.

"I've abided by my agreement. Is there some reason why you're asking?"

"Two men came to my shop and threatened me," she said.

"What men?"

"They looked like they could be connected with the mob or something."

"They weren't there on my account."

"Are you sure?"

He glared at her. "Maybe you ought to think about what you might have done to attract their attention."

"I have."

He kept his gaze on her. "And you can't think of anything?"

"No."

"You always did keep your own secrets."

"I'm not keeping secrets," she answered, but as soon as the words were out of her mouth, she knew they were a lie. She was keeping the secret of Craig Branson from her father. For several reasons. She knew he wouldn't approve, and she also knew that he wouldn't understand about what had happened between her and Branson. Nobody would understand.

Still, she managed to say, "Do you think I'd come over here and ask if you might be the cause of the problem if I already knew what was going on?"

He shrugged. "I never know what to think about you. You were usually off in your own little world—where nobody could reach you. Good luck to John Reynard. He thinks he's getting what he wants, but he's in for a surprise."

She stared at her father, hardly able to believe his words. She'd sacrificed her future to save him, and he was acting as if he didn't give a damn about her. Had his attitude toward her changed when she'd agreed to marry Reynard? Or had he seen a chance for her to do something useful for the family? And why had she agreed if this was the kind of thanks she got?

"Did I do something particular to upset you?" she asked.

"No." The word was clipped and she wondered if he was lying.

"All right," she said, then turned on her heel and left, thinking that this visit had been a waste of time.

Well, not entirely, she corrected herself. She was pretty sure that her father had nothing to do with the men who had threatened her. Which left her—where?

She shivered. She was in danger, and she could let John's men deal with the threat. Or...

Another idea was forming in her head. Craig Branson had a detective agency. Didn't that make him equipped to find out what was going on in her life that she didn't know about?

It was a logical conclusion, but she knew it was also a rationalization. She had pulled away from Branson because she'd been afraid, but now that she had some distance from him, she wanted to repeat the experience.

Which meant she had another problem. John's men were following her around. If she approached Craig Branson, they'd know it.

TOMMY LADREAU MOVED restlessly in his seat.

"You gotta pee?" his partner, Marv Strickland, asked.

"Yeah." Tommy was thinking he'd ask Marv to make a quick stop in an alley when his cell phone rang. He looked at the number, then pressed the answer button.

Marv looked at him questioningly.

Reynard, Tommy mouthed

"Report" was the crisp command from the other end of the line.

It was the man who paid him a good salary to do a wide variety of jobs—from messenger duty to surveillance to murder. Murder got his adrenaline going. Sitting around in a car keeping track of Stephanie Swift was another matter. But he always carried out his assignments to the best of his ability. He'd known all along that he was working for a dangerous man. Then Arthur Polaski had washed out of the ground in the bayou country.

It was well-known that he'd been an employee of John Reynard when he'd disappeared twenty years ago.

Reynard had been upset about the man's reappearance as a fleshless skeleton. He'd tried to keep the information quiet among the guys currently working for him, but the word had gotten around—eliciting quite a bit of speculation.

Was it the boss who'd put Polaski in the ground? Or was it someone else? Nobody knew. Nobody was happy about the discovery. And everyone was wondering—why now?

Tommy cleared his throat. "Ms. Swift left the house and went over to her father's place."

"And?"

"She stayed for about a half hour. Then she came back home, and she's been there ever since."

"And you had no problem following her?"

"No problem."

"Okay. Good. Stay on it. If anything unusual happens, I want to know about it immediately." He hesitated for a moment. "And I want to know immediately if that guy shows up. Brady. The one she claimed rescued her at the dress shop."

"Will do."

Reynard clicked off, and Tommy looked at his partner. "You hear that?"

"Yeah."

"He didn't like Brady sniffing around his honey the other night. Now he's upset about the guy showing up again at the dress shop."

"Want to bet that Brady ends up dead?" Marv asked.

Tommy shook his head. "I'm sure as Shinola not going to bet against it."

STEPHANIE SAT in her car for a few moments, trying to calm down after her meeting with her father. It was hard to believe they were related to each other. Sometimes she had fantasies about being someone else's child—and that was the reason she could never connect with him on any meaningful level.

She switched her thoughts back to Craig Branson and felt a rush of emotions—only some of them pleasant.

With a sigh, she climbed out of her car and headed for her back door. When she stepped inside, she gasped as she took in the shadowy figure sitting in the easy chair across from the door.

Chapter Six

Craig Branson watched Stephanie's security detail take off. When the car was out of sight, he crossed to the alley in back of her house and found her car missing.

They were tailing her, and either they had X-ray vision, or they had some other way to know which way she was going.

He clenched his teeth. There was no way to find out about *that* for sure until she came back.

Instead, he used his lock picks and went inside, then focused on the interior of the house, liking the mixture of antiques, comfortable chairs and sofas, and whimsical decorations.

She must like animals, because she had a lot of little ceramic, glass, wood and metal figures on the shelves among her books. He picked up a cat that looked as if it came from Mexico, stroking his fingers over the smooth, painted surface, half hoping that he'd pick up some impression of the woman herself. But he got no mental connection to her by touching any of her things.

He walked upstairs to her bedroom and stepped inside the room, loving the cool blue-and-white color scheme that reminded him of a beach cottage. His eyes zeroed in on the neatly made bed. Had John Reynard slept there with Stephanie? The thought of them naked in bed together made his throat close, and he fought to banish the image from his mind.

He wanted to linger in the bedroom, but he knew that was an invasion of her privacy.

A laugh bubbled inside him. An invasion of her privacy? Like getting into her mind? Well, that contact had invaded his privacy, too. A fair and equal invasion. He wouldn't start off their relationship by looking through her underwear drawer.

The word *relationship* stopped him. He was making assumptions. But he knew they were valid. They were going to mean something to each other. Really, they already did.

Forcing himself to turn away from the bed, he went back to the living room and sat down in one of the easy chairs to wait for her return.

Forty minutes later, he heard a car pull up outside. When he heard the lock click, his whole body tensed, and he focused like a laser on the door.

Some part of him wondered if he had imagined the intimacy between them in the dress shop. The minute she stepped into the room, he could feel the air crackling between them. If she crossed to him…if he got up and crossed to her…

He ordered himself to put away that thought.

"How did you get in here?" she demanded.

"It was easy."

He saw her lick her lips and knew that her mouth must be as dry as his.

The words she spoke weren't the ones he wanted to hear. "Don't touch me."

He felt his gaze sharpen. "Afraid?"

"Yes. You should be, too."

"Why?"

"Because…" She lifted one shoulder, apparently unwilling to put a warning into words.

He stayed where he was, but he knew that at any second he could change the rules between them by crossing the room to her, and there would be nothing she could do about it.

He felt tension course through him as he asked, "Where were you?"

"Like that's any of your business," she shot back.

When he kept his gaze fixed on her, she answered, "Visiting my father."

"To ask if he was gambling again?"

She answered with a small nod.

"What did he say?"

"He denied it."

"Which leaves you in an interesting position."

Probably she'd been considering the same thing. Instead of pursuing that line of thought, she said, "I don't appreciate finding you in here. Is this how you operate as a detective?"

"You've done some research on me?"

"Yes. I suppose you know that John Reynard has men following me around."

"Yes. I came in here after they took off after you."

She looked toward the closed venetian blinds. "They're outside now. How are you going to get out of here?"

"I'll worry about that when the time comes." He cleared his throat. "Did they show up at your father's?"

"Yes."

"Did you wonder how they knew where to pick you up?"

She swallowed. "I thought they might have some idea where I was going."

When he stood, she tensed, obviously bracing for him to come to her and put his hands on her, which was what he'd longed to do since she walked into her house. But he was going to restrain himself, at least for now.

"Maybe we'd better have a look at your car."

"My car?" she asked, obviously struggling to refocus.

"Yeah." He stood up and crossed to the door from where she'd just entered. Looking back over his shoulder, he said, "Are you coming?"

Her face was grim as she followed him, staying a few paces back when he crossed the courtyard.

At the alley, he paused and looked around. They seemed to be alone. Quickly he approached her vehicle, stooped down and felt along the edge of the bumper, then continued around the side of the car. When he found what he'd been looking for, he felt a mixture of satisfaction and annoyance.

Turning, he held out a small plastic rectangle.

She took an involuntary step closer. "What is it?"

"A GPS tracking device."

Her breath caught.

"They used that to follow you. That's why they could sit out front and wait for you to drive somewhere."

She shuddered. "What are you going to do with it?"

"Put it back."

She swallowed hard. "Why?"

"So they'll think you're still here, even if you're not."

"But…"

He shook his head. "Let's go back inside."

She stepped away, giving him room as he entered the courtyard again, then the house.

Inside, they stood in the darkened room, a feeling of anticipation zinging between them.

"Sit down," she said.

Fine, he thought. If she wanted to postpone the touching part, he'd give her some space—for now. But he could feel the need building inside him and knew that he couldn't let it go forever. He needed to find out if he'd had some kind of psychotic episode back in her shop.

He canceled that thought. He wasn't going to try to fool himself. He wasn't leaving this house without touching her.

But for the moment he lowered himself into the chair where he'd been sitting when she arrived.

She took the sofa, her wary gaze on him.

"Do you believe your father about the gambling?"

"I think so."

"Which leaves us with the question, why do you think those men showed up at your shop?"

"Do you think you can find out?"

"Yes."

"Thanks." She dragged in a breath and let it out. "You think the man I'm going to marry is responsible for your brother's death."

"You're not going to marry him," he answered, punching out the words.

She reared back. "Why not?"

"You know why not."

He'd issued a challenge. Before she could react, he was out of his chair and across the room. Pulling her to her feet, he wrapped his arms around her.

The shock of the contact made them both gasp. It was like the first time, only more intense. He knew she'd been going to ask him for information about John Reynard. Now she didn't have to ask. It was in his mind for the taking. His import-export business was a front for bringing illegal goods into the country. He had insinuated himself into New Orleans society to make his place in the city invulnerable. He had men murdered when he thought that was the best course of action.

She moaned when she saw the pictures he'd seen of the man who had been buried in the swamp for twenty years.

"Sorry," he said when words were almost impossible.

She'd told him she'd visited her father. He hadn't known how the meeting had affected her. Now he felt her pain and her bewilderment at the way her parent had just treated her.

Was it always like that? he asked.

Not as bad when my mom was alive.

I'd like to strangle him.

He's a sad old man.

That's charitable of you.

The conversation cut off as physical sensations made it difficult to focus on anything besides the two of them, the feel of his body pressed to hers and hers to his. Because both sets of sensations played through each of them.

She felt the insistence of his erection pressing against her middle, and at the same time he felt the way that part of him swelled with blood, making it difficult to form coherent thoughts.

He reached between them, cupping her breast, stroking his thumb across the hardened tip. The feel of her made him ache more painfully, and at the same time he felt her reaction, the pleasure of his cupping and stroking her and the way the sensations shot downward through her body to her center.

She gasped, rocking against him.

That's the way it is for a woman.

Yes. And for a man.

The overlay of sensations—feeling his own arousal and hers—made it almost impossible to stand as they swayed together, clinging to each other for support.

Somewhere in the back of his mind, he felt a headache building, but he ignored it. The only thing he wanted to focus on was the woman in his arms.

He wrapped her more tightly in his embrace, closing his eyes and absorbing every sensation that they shared.

He breathed in her delicious feminine scent and knew she was tuning herself to him with all her senses. Each thing they shared was magnified by the intensity of the doubled experience.

They were both breathing hard, and when she rocked her hips against his, he knew that they were heading for the bedroom. Or the sofa, because the bedroom was upstairs—too far away.

He had never felt this open to another human being.

That realization took him totally by surprise, shocking him to the marrow of his bones. All his life he had craved the closeness he had shared with his brother—searched for it—but what he felt now was more than he had experienced with Sam.

The enormity of that recognition was like a blow to his solar plexus. He dropped his hands, staggering away from Stephanie.

"Craig?"

He couldn't answer her. Not in words and not with his mind. His head was spinning as he backed up, bumping into the wall and pressing his shoulders against the vertical surface to keep his balance.

She took a step toward him, but he managed to raise one hand to ward her away.

"Don't." His voice was a harsh croak.

Her face had turned pale. Another woman would have asked what had gone wrong. But she didn't have to ask because she knew what had happened.

"I'm sorry," she whispered.

"Not your fault." He might have shaken his head, but the pain in his skull had flared to killer proportions.

Killer?

The thought had formed unbidden, but he knew it was close to the truth.

"You should sit down," she murmured.

He staggered back to the chair and flopped into the seat, throwing his head back and closing his eyes. For long moments, he struggled for equilibrium.

When he opened his eyes, he saw that she was watching him.

"You came here thinking you knew what to expect," she whispered.

"Yeah."

"You were always looking for what you had with Sam."

Again he answered in the affirmative.

"You and Sam were young." She paused, then went on, "And there was no sexual pull between you."

The statement hung in the air.

"Is it the sexual pull that brought us together?" she asked.

"It's obviously part of it," he answered, struggling to think clearly in the aftermath of the emotions that had churned through him.

"What was different about you and Sam?"

He fought to ground himself, to think about his relationship with his brother in a new way. It was a long time ago. Maybe he didn't remember it exactly as it had been.

Slowly, thinking as he spoke, he said, "We talked with thoughts, but there were other things we could do. Like if we worked together, we could move things with our minds."

"What do you mean?"

He glanced around the room and settled on the shelves along the opposite wall. "If we wanted to, we could pull a book off a shelf and drop it onto the floor without touching it."

"You and I could try that," she said, and he wondered if she was trying to get them on a different track.

"We just met today."

"No—a couple of days ago at the reception," she reminded him.

He made a huffing sound. "Yeah. There's that. But we just danced around each other there."

"Even so, we knew…something."

"True. But I don't think we're…bonded tightly enough to do any…tricks."

"I want to try," she insisted, determination in her voice.

He shrugged. "Okay, you focus on a book you want to pull off the shelf, and I'll try to help you."

He watched her turn toward the shelves and look at the titles. "There's a paperback of *The Wonderful Wizard of Oz*. That would be appropriate."

"You liked it when you were a kid?" he asked.

"Yes. Did you?"

"I liked any books that took me away from the real world."

"Well, that's something we have in common."

She walked to the shelves, found the book and pulled it a little way from the line of other books so they could both see it. Then she returned to her seat on the sofa and focused on the book. He could see the deep concentration on her face as she struggled to make something happen, and he tried to help her, giving her what he thought of as extra power. But there was no effect.

He saw sweat break out on her forehead and knew she was working as hard as she could, even though she wasn't exactly sure what she was doing. He kept up the effort to help her, but the effect was the same. Nothing.

She dragged in several breaths and sharpened her features, looking defiantly at him before turning back to the bookshelf.

Again he tried to help her, but it was clear she was only exhausting herself.

"Sorry," he murmured. "We might be able to do it if we were touching. That was the way Sam and I started out."

"If we touch, we won't end up focused on books."

He sighed. "You're probably right."

She took her lower lip between her teeth and then released it. "So why did we...open up to each other when we touched?"

"I don't know."

"What about you and Sam?"

"We always had it—whatever it is."

"I didn't. I didn't have anyone."

He heard the pain in her voice and asked the question that had been in his mind since he'd first seen her at the reception. "Did you always feel alone—like other people could connect with each other, but you couldn't?"

Her face contorted. "Yes," she whispered, and he knew it wasn't something she was sharing easily.

"I'm sorry."

"You knew there was something better."

He nodded.

"Did you have it with anyone besides Sam?"

"No."

"Then the big question is—why us?"

Chapter Seven

Stephanie waited for Craig's answer.

"There must be something we have in common." He shifted in his seat. "We might find out what it is if we touch each other again."

She stared at him, tempted by the suggestion, heat shooting through her as she remembered where they'd been a few minutes ago. He'd pulled away from her when he realized that what they were building between them was more intense than what he'd had with his brother. Now he was ready to try again, and she was the one who was feeling cautious.

"I think it would be better to do it the old-fashioned way. I mean talking. You researched me. Did you find anything that was similar?"

He shrugged. "Okay, if you want to play Twenty Questions. We're about the same age. But what else do we have in common?"

"Not our location. You grew up in the D.C. area, and I always lived down here."

He nodded. "What we're looking for could be anything. From chemicals in the air to the treatments we got on our teeth, to the medicines we took, to the food we ate."

She made a low sound. "I suppose neither one of us was near a nuclear test site."

"I guess not. And it was early for oil spills to contaminate Gulf seafood."

"Nice of you to think of that, but that wouldn't have applied to you, anyway. Anything strange about the food you ate? I mean, were your parents on any kind of health-food kick?"

"Actually, they were on a low-carb kick for a long time."

"But you had gone out for Italian food and take-home pizza," she said, then regretted the reference to his brother's murder.

His face clouded. "That was a special treat."

"I'm sorry."

He lifted one shoulder. "It will keep coming up."

She focused on the original question. "Well, it's definitely not from low carbs. I ate a pretty normal American diet—with Cajun touches because we lived down here. So that's not it."

"What about mental illness in your family?"

"What's that got to do with it?"

"This has something to do with our brains. Maybe you can only do it if you're schizophrenic," he muttered.

"You really think that?"

"No. But something else, maybe."

"If you dig around enough, you find out that everyone has a relative that was 'off.' You have an uncle Charlie who was committed?" she asked.

"When he came back from Vietnam and was never quite right again. What about you?"

"I guess my mother's sister suffered from depression. They didn't talk about it much."

"Okay, what about physical illnesses? Anything unusual?"

"No, what about you?" she asked.

"I had all the vaccinations."

"I did, too. But people have suspected vaccinations of causing various problems—like autism."

"I suppose," he allowed. "I wonder what our moms ate when they were pregnant with us."

The question made her mind zing back to something she remembered, and she cleared her throat. "There is something else. I once heard my parents talking about how hard it was for my mom to get pregnant."

He went very still. "And she had some kind of treatment?"

"I think she went to a fertility clinic."

"That's interesting. Mine did, too," he said slowly. "A friend of hers who lived in New Orleans told her about a doctor who was supposed to be very good, and she traveled to Louisiana to see him."

They stared at each other. "To New Orleans?"

"I don't know. Do you think that could be it?"

"It's something unusual," he conceded.

"What clinic?"

"I don't know."

"Would your father know the name of the place?"

A MAN NAMED Harold Goddard could have given them the answer—if he'd been so inclined.

But he wasn't the kind of man who did things simply because they were in the best interests of others. His moves were always careful and calculated. He was cautious when it came to his own welfare, yet the quest for knowledge was a powerful motivator. Not just knowledge for its own sake. He wanted information he could use to his advantage.

This afternoon he was waiting for a report from New Orleans regarding a scenario that he'd set in motion a couple of months ago.

He turned from the window and walked to his desk,

where he scrolled through the messages in his email. Unfortunately, there was nothing he hadn't known a few hours ago.

With a sigh, he got up and left the office, heading for his home gym, which was equipped with a treadmill, a recumbent bike and a universal weight machine. This afternoon he stepped onto the treadmill and slowly raised the speed to three miles per hour.

He was in his sixties, and he hated to exercise, but he knew that it was supposed to keep his body fit and his mind sharp, so he made himself do it.

He was retired now, but he kept up his interest in the projects that he'd handled for the Howell Institute, working under the direction of a man named Bill Wellington, who'd operated with funds hidden in a variety of budget entries. Wellington had been interested in advancing America through the application of science. Everything from new ways to fertilize crops to schemes for improving the human race.

Some of the experiments were well thought out, others bordered on lunatic fringe. And all of them had been shut down years ago. Or at least Goddard had thought so—until a few months ago when the news from Houma, Louisiana, had been filled with reports of an explosion in a private research laboratory. The local fire marshal had ruled that the explosion was due to a gas leak, but Goddard had sent his own team down to investigate, and he suspected there might be another explanation—because the clinic had been owned by a Dr. Douglas Solomon. He'd been one of Wellington's fair-haired boys, until his experiments had failed to pan out.

Solomon had operated a fertility clinic in Houma, Louisiana, where he'd been highly successful in using in vitro fertilization techniques. It was what he'd tried with the embryos that had not been a roaring success. Solomon's experiments had been designed to produce children with superintelligence, but when his testing of the subjects had not shown they had higher IQs than would be expected in a normal bell curve, the Howell Institute had terminated the funding.

But now the children had reached adulthood, and there might be something important the doctor and Wellington had both missed—as demonstrated by the mysterious explosion in Houma.

Goddard had partial records from the Solomon Clinic, and he'd followed up on some of the children. A number of them had disappeared. Others had died under mysterious circumstances—often in bed together—around the country.

But had Solomon unwittingly created men and women with something special that had previously been latent—until they made contact with each other?

Because he wanted to know the answer to that question, he'd decided to try an experiment. After scrolling through the list of names, he'd found two that looked as if they were perfect for his purposes. Stephanie Swift and Craig Branson.

He'd set in motion a scenario that had propelled them together. Now he was waiting to find out the effects. But he couldn't afford to leave them on the loose for long. And what he did when he captured them was still up for consideration. He'd like to know what they could do together, but it might also be important to examine their brain tissues.

STEPHANIE LOOKED DOWN at her hands. "I don't know if my dad remembers the name of the clinic, and I don't know if he'd tell me if he did. He wasn't too friendly when I went over there this afternoon."

"Why not?"

"Maybe he's feeling guilty about my agreeing to marry John to pay his gambling debts—and he's showing it by acting angry with me."

"That doesn't make perfect sense."

She sighed. "And I did accuse him of gambling again, which didn't go over too well."

"Yeah, right."

"How did you get along with your parents?" she asked.

"They knew I was devastated by Sam's death. They tried to make it up to me. I let them think they were succeeding."

"But it didn't really work?"

"It couldn't. The other half of me was…gone."

When her face contorted, he said, "Let's not focus on that."

"Okay, are your parents both still alive?"

His features tightened. "Neither of them is alive. Sam's death did a number on our family. My mom was depressed—like your aunt. But it didn't develop until after Sam died. She died of a heart attack. And my dad started drinking a lot. He died of cirrhosis of the liver."

"I'm sorry."

He shrugged. "I felt like I was on my own a long time before they were actually gone."

She nodded.

"I didn't keep much of their stuff. If there's information about the clinic, the information is back in Bethesda. Do you think your father will tell you what clinic?"

"I don't know. There are probably some old records we could find if he doesn't want to talk to me."

"We should go over there."

She glanced toward the window, then got up and lifted one of the slats. "My bodyguards are still here."

"They can sit there all night. We'll leave your car in the

parking space out back, walk to my bed-and-breakfast and get my rental."

"Okay."

It was strange to be sneaking away from her own house, but she followed Craig out the door, across the patio and into the back alley. Bypassing the car, they headed for his B and B. He checked to make sure they weren't being followed and kept to the shadows of the wrought-iron balconies that sheltered the sidewalk.

He stopped down the block and across the street, still in the shadows. "The parking lot is around back. You wait here. I don't want anyone to see you with me when I get the car."

She quickly agreed, pressing back against the building as she watched him cross the street and disappear into the B and B.

In a few minutes, a late-model Impala pulled up at the curb, and she climbed in, shutting the door quickly behind her.

"I suppose you know where my dad lives," she said as he pulled back into the traffic lane.

"Yeah."

As they drove out of the French Quarter, then to St. Charles Avenue, Craig kept glancing in his rearview mirror, making sure that nobody was following them.

"I guess you're used to this cloak-and-dagger stuff," Stephanie murmured.

"Part of my job description."

As he headed up St. Charles, then turned onto St. Andrew Street, her heart started to pound. She hadn't exactly had a pleasant encounter with her father, and she hadn't expected to meet up with him again so soon.

"You get out. I'm going to leave the car around the corner," he said as he pulled up in front of the house.

"I'll wait for you outside."

He gave her a critical look. "You really don't want to be here, do you?"

"No. And I'm thinking that it's not so great for you."

"Because?"

"Because he's given me to John Reynard, and he's not going to be happy to see me with another man."

"*Given* is a pretty strong word."

She shot him a fierce look. "You don't think I agreed to marry Reynard because I was madly in love, do you?"

"No. I thought you were interested in his money."

She dragged in a sharp breath. "Thanks."

"I didn't know you then."

"And now you do?"

"You can't lie with your thoughts."

"At least that's something."

He turned his head toward her, then looked back to the road. "I'm working my way through this situation—just the way you are."

"You've had some experience with it."

"This is different." He waited a beat before saying, "To get back to the current problem, tell your father I'm a detective you've hired to find out who the men were."

"He'll think John could handle that on his own."

Craig shrugged. "Do you have a better idea?"

"No."

Stephanie climbed out of the car and walked up the driveway toward the detached garage. When she looked inside and saw that her father's car was missing, she breathed a little sigh of relief, then started wondering where he was.

Because she said she'd be outside, she waited for Craig on the wide front porch.

"It looks like my dad isn't home," she said.

"Good."

"I hope so. He doesn't like…" She stopped.

"What."

"…me sneaking around."

"What the hell does that mean? This is your house."

"Not anymore. I moved out."

"Your father sounds like a real winner."

"He's had…a hard life."

"Oh, come on."

"He was used to wealth and privilege, and he lost that."

"His own fault," Craig pointed out.

"Maybe that makes it worse."

"Do you always make excuses for him?"

"Let's not go on about him," she snapped, and he pressed his lips together, maybe because he realized he would gain nothing by continuing to focus on her father's failings.

After she unlocked the door, she turned to him. "Come inside, but wait in the front hall."

"I should check out the house."

"For what?"

"Intruders."

"Unlikely."

To her relief, he stayed in the hall while she darted into the living room, then circled through the rest of the downstairs before climbing quickly up the stairs.

Leaning over the balcony, she beckoned to him. "Come on."

"WHAT ARE WE looking for?" he asked when he reached the top of the stairs.

"I'm not sure. It was almost thirty years ago, so it's not going to be on the computer, but Mom kept some boxes with papers and pictures in the top of her closet."

Craig followed her into a bedroom where the furnishings

were antique and the once-expensive fabrics were dusty and faded.

"Your dad sleeps here?" he asked.

"This was Mom's room."

"They had separate rooms?"

"She told him about fifteen years ago that she needed her own space," Stephanie answered, embarrassed to be revealing private family matters.

The room had two large closets, both full of women's clothes.

When Stephanie saw them, she caught her breath.

"Everything's still right where she left it," she murmured.

"I guess he misses her. Or he didn't feel like making the effort to get rid of her stuff. All he had to do was shut the door."

She dragged in a breath and let it out. "I feel funny about poking around in their lives."

"Yeah, but we need to do it," Craig answered. "Are those what you're looking for?" He pointed to the cardboard boxes neatly stacked on the top shelf. They were old department-store boxes, the kind nobody made anymore.

"Yes."

He lifted several down and set them on the bed.

Instead of reaching for them, Stephanie stood unmoving.

Craig turned his head toward her. "I know this is making you feel…unsettled."

She nodded. "And Dad is going to be mad if he comes back and finds me snooping."

"I guess that's tough. But maybe we can get out of here before he comes back. Do you want me to help you look?"

"Yes. Thanks."

They each opened a box and began checking through

the contents. Inside were old photographs of Stephanie and her parents, plus other memorabilia.

Craig held up a childish crayoned picture of a house surrounded by a flower garden. "You did good work."

"I must have been pretty young. It's a drawing of this house."

"I actually can tell."

She found a pile of essays she'd written.

"It's strange to find this stuff. I wouldn't have thought she'd kept it."

Craig said nothing, only continued searching through papers. When he pulled out a thick folder, she looked at him. "What's that?"

He thumbed through the contents.

"Do you remember anything about a place called the Solomon Clinic?"

"What is it?"

"Maybe this is what we've been looking for. It was a fertility clinic in Houma. There's a copy of an application, then instruction sheets for what your mother was supposed to do before going there."

He handed her some of the papers, and she went through them. "I guess this is it."

"Well, we found out about me. Does the Solomon name mean anything to you?" she asked.

Craig considered the question. "As a matter of fact, it does."

"How?"

His stomach tightened as he said, "Like you, I used to listen in on conversations. Probably all kids do."

"And what did you hear?"

"It was after Sam died, and my mother was pretty upset. I think I heard her on the phone trying to get some information about the Solomon Clinic."

"You really remember that?"

"Yes, because of the way she was reacting. In her grief, I think she might have been considering trying to get pregnant again, but she found out that the clinic had burned down."

"She could have gone to someone in the D.C. area."

"Maybe she thought Dr. Solomon was God—and he was the only one who could help her. For all I know, he could have acted that way with his patients." He dragged in a breath and let it out. "Anyway, she apparently gave up on the idea."

"But it sounds like your mother and mine went to the same place," Stephanie said. "Only she didn't take you back there for checkups, did she?"

"You went for checkups?" he asked.

"Yes. I remembered going *somewhere* with a waiting room full of kids my age. Now I think it must have been part of the deal—that the parents would bring the kids back to be examined."

"And my mom was back in D.C., so she couldn't do it." He thought for a minute. "I wonder if she agreed to take me and Sam there for checkups, but then didn't comply," Craig said.

"Was she that kind of woman?"

He lifted one shoulder. "She was always willing to bend the rules when it suited her."

"Can you give me an example?"

"I was supposed to have Ms. Franklin for my sixth-grade homeroom teacher. Mom got me into a different class because she thought Ms. Franklin was too lenient with the kids. Another time we moved into an apartment building where you weren't supposed to have pets, but she brought our cat anyway. Lucky for her it was a well-behaved animal and didn't mess up the place."

They gathered up the papers and put them back into the boxes, then returned the containers to the top of the closet.

"Your mom found out the clinic closed," she said.

"But maybe we can find out something online—or if we go to Houma."

Stephanie turned to straighten out the bedspread, where they'd laid the boxes, and he took the other side, pulling to remove the wrinkles.

"If we get out of here before your dad comes back, he'll never even know we were here."

They hadn't finished smoothing out the bed when they heard the front door open.

"What do you want to do?" Craig asked in a harsh whisper.

"Climb out the window," Stephanie answered in the same tone.

"You're kidding."

She shook her head. "I don't want Dad to find me upstairs with you, and I don't want to get into an argument about what we were doing—not if I can help it. And I sure as heck don't want him telling John about it."

"We're on the second floor."

"But there's an easy way to get down. We can climb onto the sunroom roof and go down that way." She hurried toward the window, opened the sash and stepped out. Craig looked around to make sure nothing was out of place in the room, then he followed her onto the roof. When he was outside, he closed the window behind them.

They moved along the wall toward the edge of the sunroom, and Stephanie pointed to the trellises that were fixed to the walls of the sunroom.

"Let me go first," he said.

"No, I've done this before."

"You snuck out of the house?"

"When I was grounded, yeah. The trellis is as good as a ladder."

"But you haven't used it in years, right?"

She shrugged. Before he could stop her, she stepped over the side, holding on to the weathered wood as she began to lower herself. He watched her going down, thinking that the wood might not be as solid as when she'd tried this last.

His speculation was confirmed when he heard a cracking sound and she fell several feet before catching herself.

"Are you all right?" he called.

"Yes."

When she'd made it to the ground, he followed, testing the rungs as he went. The rest seemed solid, and he reached the lawn right after Stephanie.

They stared at each other. He would have hugged her in relief that they'd made it, but he knew that touching her now was a bad idea. They'd forget what they were supposed to be doing—which was getting away from her father's house before he discovered them.

She must have been thinking the same thing. After long seconds, she walked rapidly across the back of the house and turned the corner.

As soon as she disappeared from sight, he heard her make a strangled sound.

"Stephanie?" he called in a hoarse whisper.

She didn't answer, and he hurried to catch up, then stopped short when he rounded the corner.

Stephanie was standing rigidly in front of a man who was holding a gun to her head.

Chapter Eight

The man was one of the thugs who had threatened Stephanie in her shop. The bald one.

"If you don't want me to shoot your girlfriend, do exactly what I say."

Craig went still as he looked from the man to Stephanie's terrified face.

"Don't hurt her."

"That's up to you. Play this smart, and everything will be okay."

He doubted it, but he asked, "What do you want?"

Without answering the question, the man said, "Walk ahead of us down the driveway, then turn right."

Craig's heart was pounding as he followed directions. He walked carefully, knowing that any false step could get Stephanie killed.

As they headed down the sidewalk, he kept searching for a way out. What if a neighbor suddenly appeared? What if someone called the police? Craig prayed that *something* would happen. The big problem for him was that Stephanie and the guy were behind him, and he couldn't see what was going on back there. If he moved on his own, she'd get shot.

Desperately he tried to reach out to her with his mind, but he couldn't make the contact across the space that separated them.

"Stop here," the guy ordered as they drew up beside a van that could have been a delivery truck. The only windows were in the front and in the back door. The rest of the rear compartment had solid walls.

The other man, the one with the wavy hair, opened the door at the back of the vehicle. "Get inside," he ordered.

Craig hesitated, thinking that if he followed directions, he'd never gain control of the situation.

"I said get in." The man behind him gave him a shove, and he flew forward, striking his head against the bare metal floor of the interior compartment.

His head hit the floor so hard that he saw stars. Behind him, he heard Stephanie cry out.

"Shut up," the man with the gun growled.

Craig fought to stay conscious as the man flipped him onto his back and pulled his hands behind him, quickly securing them with tape. He did the same with his legs, then rolled him back over and banged his head again, sending a wave of pain through his skull.

"Easy," the other guy complained. "We're supposed to deliver them in good shape."

"Yeah, well, that's for mauling me this afternoon," the curly-haired one answered while he tore off more tape and slapped it over Craig's mouth.

He was still trying to clear his mind as the bald-headed man shoved Stephanie into the van.

She gasped as he pushed her to the floor, then began taping her the way Craig was already taped.

He was silently screaming, racking his brain for some way out of this, but he could come up with nothing.

When both of them were secured, the men climbed out of the van and slammed the door closed, leaving their prisoners in the dark.

Craig struggled to think clearly, struggled to send Stephanie a silent message, but he couldn't reach her mind.

As the vehicle lurched away from the curb, he sensed Stephanie moving beside him. Through the fog in his brain, he realized that she was wiggling her body closer to his. Finally her right shoulder and arm were pressed to his left.

He felt her fear and also a spurt of hope as his thoughts collided with hers.

Are you all right? she asked urgently.

Yeah, he answered, knowing that she immediately picked up on the lie.

She rolled so that her body was half on top of his, and they pressed more tightly together. When she moved her cheek against his, he longed to raise his arms and fold her close. But the tape prevented that.

Still, as he absorbed the physical and the mental contact with her, he felt a profound sense of relief.

I'm sorry, she whispered in his mind.

For what?

For rushing out the window.

You thought your father was coming in.

Now I don't even know. Was it him—or them?

He had no answer, but he was thankful for the strong mental link that was letting them speak directly to each other.

What matters now is escape.

Who are these men?

No idea. But we have to get away from them, he repeated, trying not to think of horrible possibilities. Unfortunately, he knew Stephanie was picking them up from his mind.

We have to get this tape off.

How?

Remember when you were trying to move that book?

It didn't work.

Because we weren't touching. We are now.

He tried to send reassurances along with the silent words. It would have worked better if his head wasn't throbbing from the banging against the floor of the van.

I'm going to work on the tape on my hands.

How?

I'm going to stretch it. You send me energy. I can't explain exactly what that means. Just...maybe focus on what I'm doing.

He hadn't done anything like this in years, and with Sam, it had always been for fun. Now his and Stephanie's lives might depend on it.

When he heard her wince, he wished he had kept away from that last thought.

The van lurched, and he lost his concentration for a moment. He gritted his teeth as he struggled to focus. He had met Stephanie Swift only a few days ago, and he expected her to help him with a mental task that seemed impossible on the face of it.

We can do it. She answered the unspoken thought.

He made a sound of agreement, not because he was entirely confident but because they had no choice. They had to get out of this mess.

The pounding in his head made focusing difficult, but he kept at it. For minutes, nothing seemed to happen. Finally he felt some small measure of success—a tiny loosening of the bindings on his wrists.

Stephanie must have noticed it, too, because he felt her spurt of hope.

He worked at the tape. It seemed to take centuries, but finally he could part his wrists a little.

He was almost too mentally exhausted to continue, but

he kept at it, feeling the tape loosen more and more, and finally he was able to wiggle his hands free.

He glanced toward the front of the van and was relieved to see that the two men were both facing forward.

Reaching for Stephanie, he began to slowly pull the tape off her wrists. It was easier to work manually, and he quickly got her hands free. She breathed out a small sigh and pulled her legs up so that she could remove the tape from her ankles. He did the same.

When his hands and legs were free, he eased the tape off his mouth, seeing that she was doing that, too.

Thank God, she whispered into his mind.

He thought about their next move. They were free of the tape, but they were still in a moving van. He looked around for something he could use as a weapon and saw nothing. Too bad he'd gotten rid of the gun that he'd taken from these guys.

We can't fight them.

What are we going to do?

Hope they have to stop at a light.

He glanced at the men in front who were paying no attention to the prisoners. Obviously they thought that the man and woman they'd restrained were no threat.

Praying that neither of their kidnappers decided to check on them, Craig inched his way toward the back of the vehicle. Pausing again, he checked on the gunmen. When he saw they were still facing forward, he pulled down on the handle, easing the door open a crack so that he could see out. He was relieved to find they were still in the city—but not a part he recognized.

Stephanie picked up her purse, which had been lying beside her, and slung the strap across her chest before moving to the back of the van with him, her shoulder pressed to his.

Get ready.

Their chance came when the van lurched to a stop again. He pushed the door open and leaped out, then reached to help Stephanie down. They were on a city street with cars immediately behind them.

"Where are we?"

"The financial district."

They heard an angry shout and turned to see Curly, the one in the van's passenger seat, jump out with his gun drawn.

"Come on," Craig said to Stephanie, taking her hand. They wove through the traffic, the maneuver creating a blast of honking horns. As a car came around the corner and almost plowed into them, the driver slammed on the brakes, then lowered his window and started cursing at them.

Ignoring the chaos, they kept running for their lives through the darkened streets as pedestrians stared at the scene. And the car that had almost hit them gave them cover for a moment.

As they ran, Craig looked around wildly, trying to figure out the best escape route.

It was Stephanie who took the lead. "This way," she shouted, darting down a dark passageway between two tall buildings.

Craig followed. He wanted to look behind him to see if the guy with the gun knew where they'd gone, but turning would slow them down.

Stephanie pulled on a side door. It opened and they stepped into a hallway.

They ran down to the first turn and dodged around the corner. Finally, risking a quick look back, Craig saw the gunman charging after them.

Instead of continuing the evasive action, Craig waited for the man to come barreling down the hall, then stuck out his foot, tripping the guy and sending him sprawling. Craig was on him in an instant, grabbing his hair and slamming his face against the tile floor, thinking that turnabout was fair play. The man gasped and went still.

Craig lifted the gun from the man's limp hand and shoved it into the waistband of his jeans, then covered it with his knit shirt. When he searched the man's pockets, he found no identification.

"We'd better get out of here."

"Don't you want to ask him why they're after us?"

"Yeah, but his partner could show up at any moment. We have to put distance between us and them."

She answered with a tight nod and followed him to a glass-enclosed lobby.

They stepped out into a plaza surrounded by office buildings.

Walking rapidly, they crossed to the opposite side, then back to the street. When Craig saw a taxi heading their way in the curb lane, he hailed it.

"Where to?" the cabbie asked.

Craig gave the address where he'd left his car.

As the vehicle took off, he scanned the street for the van and the men who had taken them prisoner, but neither was in sight.

When Stephanie started to speak, Craig squeezed her hand.

Not here.

She clamped her lips together and knit her fingers with his.

They were both breathing hard from the chase and the narrow escape. And now that the crisis was over, he could feel the sexual pull starting to surge between them.

Touching her made him want her, but the physical connection also seemed to strengthen the silent communication they'd first discovered in the dress shop. If they had been in a hotel instead of a cab, he would have taken her directly to the check-in desk and booked a room.

She caught the thought and glanced at him, then away.

"Sorry," he muttered. "It's a guy thing."

Not just a guy thing, apparently.

We have to find a safe place where we can figure out what's going on.

You think we can do it?

I hope so.

The cab pulled onto the street near her father's house where he'd left his car, but he asked the driver to stop half-way down the block.

The guy pulled to the curb, and they got out.

After paying the man, Craig motioned Stephanie into the shadows of an overhanging pepper tree. "Wait here."

"Why?"

"They could have staked out my car."

"If they know where it is."

"We can't assume we're in the clear."

She waited while he walked swiftly down the block, all his senses on alert, but nobody approached the car. It could be that the men didn't even know this was his rental. When he gestured for Stephanie to follow, she hurried down the block and climbed into the passenger seat.

He'd kept their physical contact to a minimum. But now they were off the street, and when she turned to him, he reached for her, feeling emotions flowing between them. Relief that they had made their escape, coupled with the sexual need intensifying between them. And, under that, the uncertainty about their situation—on so many levels.

He lowered his mouth to hers for a kiss that left them both gasping. He knew they should drive away because their attackers could come back. But he couldn't turn her loose, not yet. Everything inside him had gone cold when he'd seen that gun pressed to her head. He'd been scared spitless—for her. And he'd realized in that moment that he couldn't lose her.

He knew she took in his thoughts. Wrenching her mouth from his, she stared at him.

Yes, she whispered in his mind, telling him the same thing. She couldn't lose him.

How could I have gotten engaged to John Reynard?

You didn't know what he was.

It's more than that. If I'd married him, I would have tried to make the best of it. But that was before I knew you.

He tightened his arms around her. A while ago, he had been unable to comprehend a relationship stronger than the one he'd had with Sam. Now he was starting to understand the depths of what he had found with Stephanie. The link between them had gotten them out of that van—maybe saved their lives.

But we need...

To be closer.

Just allowing that thought sent a surge of arousal through him, yet he eased his body away from her.

We have to find a safe place where we can...

Make love, she finished for him.

"Yeah," he said aloud.

"My family has a cabin out in bayou country, near New Iberia. We can go there."

He let the picture of the isolated cabin fill his mind. They'd be alone, uninterrupted.

"Does Reynard know about it?"

"I don't think so."

He nodded, deciding he'd make a judgment about the hideout later. "Right now, I need to get my laptop from my bed-and-breakfast."

She tightened her hand on his. "Isn't that dangerous?"

"It's dangerous for my hard drive to fall into enemy hands."

"Enemy hands. You mean Reynard—or whoever those men are working for?"

"Right. Either one."

"What do they want with us?" she asked in a strained voice.

"I don't know, but we'd better find out."

"I know it's a stretch, but do you think it has something to do with…that clinic?"

"Someone who wants to hurt John could be after you."

"He didn't share that with me if it's true. And they came after both of us."

"Well, they could be mad that I rescued you."

"Okay. Right."

"On the other hand, they could have just killed me and left me there—then taken you in the van. But they took both of us."

She sucked in a sharp breath.

"But back to your question about that clinic. You have to wonder why they wanted to keep testing the children." Deliberately he took his hand away from hers.

She leaned back against the seat with her eyes closed.

Hell of a day, he said.

Hard to imagine, she answered.

His head jerked toward her. "We weren't touching."

Her eyes widened. "That's right."

"But we spoke mind to mind."

Yes.

"We have to strengthen that skill."

"Yes," she answered again. "We have to see how far apart we can get and still do it." She turned her head toward him. "Did you and Sam have to be touching to speak mind to mind?"

"At first we did. Then later we could do it farther and farther apart."

Excitement bubbled inside him as he contemplated the possibilities, but he ruthlessly cut off those thoughts. The first thing he had to do was make sure they were safe. From Reynard and from whoever else was after them.

"Why haven't you reported in?" John Reynard asked the men he had stationed outside Stephanie's house.

"Nothing to report," Tommy Ladreau replied. "She's still home."

"How do you know?"

"Her car is still where she left it when she came home from her father's."

John considered that assessment. He would have called the shop if it had still been open. Was she still holed up in her house?

The tracking device he'd had the men put on her car showed the vehicle hadn't moved. But what if she'd left on foot. Or—in another car?

That question brought to mind the man who'd been stalking her. Craig Brady. There was no information about him, which probably meant that Craig Brady wasn't his real name.

"Give her another hour," he said, "then go knock on the door and tell her you're just checking in."

He got off the phone and called a man in the police force who often did some work for him.

"This is John Reynard," he said when his contact picked up.

"Yes?" came the cautious reply.

"There was an incident at Stephanie Swift's clothing boutique earlier today."

"Like what?"

"Two men came in and threatened her, and another guy charged in afterward and fought them off."

"Okay."

"I want you to go over there and dust for fingerprints. I want to know who those men were."

"I can't do it right away."

"I think you'd better drop what you're doing and get busy," he said, then hung up.

CRAIG DROVE BACK to the French Quarter and found a parking space around the corner from his bed-and-breakfast. He would have told Stephanie to wait in the car, but he knew from her thoughts that she wasn't going to let him go back there alone.

They held hands, trying to look casual as they kept to the sides of the buildings, heading back toward the antebellum mansion where he was staying. But all his senses were on alert as he scanned the area around them. Before they reached the mansion, he spotted one of the men who had kidnapped them, waiting in the shadows across the street. It was the bald guy.

Stephanie caught Craig's thought and went still, then followed his gaze.

The man was looking toward the house, and they were able to back up and around the corner.

"We have to get out of here."

"I need my computer."

"That's too dangerous."

"Let me think." He laughed softly. "Too bad we can't convince him we're invisible."

"Oh, sure."

He shrugged. "It's worth considering."

She stared at him. "You think we could do something like that?"

"I think we may have a lot of possibilities we can explore. But not until we can get out of the city."

He knew she wanted to ask him to give up on his computer, but he wasn't willing to do it—not with so much data in it. Of course, it was password-protected, but an expert could probably hack his way in.

"If this guy is out front, you can assume the other one is at the back."

"Yeah."

"Let's check that out."

They reversed their steps, heading back to the alley on the perpendicular street. Staying close to the buildings, they walked quietly toward the mansion. They spotted the curly-haired man in the yard across the street before he spotted them. As Stephanie stared at him, she took Craig's hand.

He caught his breath when he saw what she had in mind. "No."

Chapter Nine

"No," Craig repeated.

"You have a better idea?" Stephanie asked as she scanned the alley, which was empty of people.

When he couldn't come up with one, she said, "There's a drugstore in the block back there. Let's go get some duct tape."

"You like the idea of poetic justice?"

"You know I do."

They went back for the tape, then separated. Stephanie walked to the end of the alley where they'd entered before, and Craig went the other way. When they had visual contact with each other, she started walking down the alley as though she wasn't aware that she was in any danger. Craig hurried to get into position.

As she'd predicted, the man saw her and stepped out of the backyard where he'd been hiding, his gun in his hand.

Stephanie stopped and gasped.

As the man closed in on her, Craig rushed behind him. The thug must have heard him, because he whirled. Before he could fire, Stephanie pushed him to the side, throwing him off balance. Craig brought the butt of his gun down on the man's head, and he collapsed.

After looking around to make sure nobody was watching, they pulled his limp body into the backyard where he'd been hiding and quickly taped his hands and feet, the way they'd been taped in the van. His face was already battered and bruised from when Craig had slammed his head against the floor.

He groaned, and Craig shook him. His eyes blinked open. For seconds they were clouded with confusion before he focused on his captors.

"Who are you working for?" Craig asked as he crouched over the captive.

Curly's only answer was a feral glare.

Craig slapped him across his bruised face, and he gasped. "Who?"

The man looked desperate, but he answered, "I don't know."

"Nice try."

"It's the truth. We was hired by phone."

"How did they know to contact you?"

"I guess we got a reputation."

Craig snorted. "Okay, I can buy that. Where were you supposed to take us?"

"To the parking lot of a shopping center in Thibodaux."

Craig sighed. If it was true, it was an arrangement designed to reveal the least possible information if this guy was apprehended.

"We got away from you. Did you tell your client?"

"Yeah."

Craig fired more questions at their captive. "And what did he say?"

"He sent us here."

"It's a man?"

"Yes. At least I think so, unless it's a woman using one of those fancy things that distort your voice."

Craig sighed. "Why did he want us?"

"He didn't say."

"So you have a number to call. What is it?"

"I can't tell you."

Craig raised his hand, and the man cringed, then spit out a number. Stephanie pulled a pen and paper from her purse and wrote it down.

Figuring he'd gotten what he could, Craig slapped a piece of tape over the man's mouth, then handed the captured gun to Stephanie. "Keep him covered."

While she held the gun in a two-handed grip, Craig went through the man's pockets. This time he found a wallet and a cell phone, which he took.

The man made an angry sound as Craig took the money from the wallet. There were no credit cards or identification.

"I'll be back in a couple of minutes. Keep him covered."

He knew she didn't want to be left alone with the guy, but she didn't voice the complaint as he hurried to the back door of the bed-and-breakfast.

Was he making a mistake coming back here?

He hoped not.

Cautiously he opened the door and scanned the back hall, but it was empty. Still ready for trouble, he climbed to the second floor and tested the knob on his door. It was still locked, and he inserted the key.

To his relief, it looked as if nobody had been in the room since he'd left it that morning. He threw his computer into a carry bag and grabbed the suitcase that he'd left packed. Two minutes after he'd entered the room, he was on his way out.

As he ran back down the alley, he cast his mind ahead of him. At first he heard nothing mental, then about twenty yards from where he'd left Stephanie with the thug, his thoughts suddenly collided with hers.

Thank God.

Everything's fine.

She answered with a silent laugh. *I guess that's relative.*

The guy glared at them as Craig stepped into the backyard. "Let's get the hell out of here."

The man on the ground stared bullets at their back as Craig hurried Stephanie away.

"Can we stop at my house?" she asked.

TOMMY LADREAU HEAVED himself out of the car and stretched.

He'd been watching Stephanie Swift's house for hours, and he was sure he wasn't going to find out anything new by knocking on her door.

But those were his orders, so he ambled across the street and knocked.

When there was no answer, he looked back toward his partner.

Marv Strickland got out of the car and joined him.

"Now what?"

"Let's see if her car's really there."

They walked around to the back of the house. The vehicle was still sitting where Stephanie had left it when she'd come home.

They exchanged glances, then crossed the enclosed patio and knocked on the side door. Still no response.

Marv pulled out his cell phone and called their boss.

"Stephanie Swift's car is here, but she's not answering her door. What do you want us to do?"

There was a long silence before Reynard answered.

CRAIG SIGHED. "We're already pressing our luck. You can pick up some clothes at a discount department store outside of town."

"It would be a lot more efficient for me to just take some stuff from my house."

He thought about it, knowing that she'd be more comfortable with her own things. "If you're quick," he finally said.

They drove toward her house, and he slowed as he came to the cross street. The car where the two men had been watching the house was still there, but he couldn't see anyone inside.

"Duck down," he said to Stephanie.

She slid lower in her seat as he turned the corner and drove by the car. It was empty, but as he drew abreast of her front door, it opened, and one of the men who had been in the vehicle stepped out. He saw Craig, and their eyes met.

Craig swore under his breath and stamped on the accelerator. The man shouted to his partner, who also dashed out of the house. Both of them ran for their vehicle as Craig sped away.

Stephanie popped up in her seat, trying to see what was going on.

"Stay down," he shouted, but he had the feeling the damage was already done.

He wove through the French Quarter, trying to avoid pedestrians. A truck pulled in front of them, blocking their way.

Craig leaned on the horn. Stephanie looked in back of them and dragged in a strangled breath. When he looked in the rearview mirror, he could see the car gaining on them. It pulled up behind them, and one of the bodyguards jumped out.

"Make sure your door is locked," Craig shouted.

Stephanie pressed the button seconds before the man reached her side of the vehicle and yanked on the door handle.

Just then the truck moved a couple of feet, giving Craig

room to maneuver around it by putting his left wheels on the sidewalk.

"Turn down the alley," Stephanie told him.

He took her advice, turning right and heading for the next street. They came out on Esplanade, and he turned right again. Although the bodyguards were no longer in back of them, he kept up a circuitous route through the city, thankful that there was no tracking device on his rental.

"They saw me with you," Stephanie whispered. "They'll tell John."

"You can say I kidnapped you."

"Oh, sure."

"It could be true."

"That guy saw me lock my door."

"Maybe I was holding a gun on you."

She clenched her hands into fists.

"Sorry," he murmured.

"What do you want to do?" he asked, his breath frozen in his chest.

She swung her head toward him. "I don't want to go back to John Reynard, if that's what you're asking."

He managed to breathe.

She reached for his hand, and he felt the mental connection they'd established—and sensed her thoughts. Her fear of John Reynard. Her relief that she'd escaped. Her fear that perhaps she'd jumped from the frying pan into the fire.

Yeah, he silently answered.

So now what?

I think we'd better not go to your cabin. Give me some other suggestions.

Houma?

The other guys could be looking for us there.

She named another town. "It's about twenty miles from Houma."

"That should work."

As they drove away from the city, he felt a mixture of emotions. He'd found a woman who shared a bond with him that was stronger than anything he'd ever experienced, but that might be the reason someone was trying to capture them.

She caught the thought. *Sorry.*

We'll deal with it.

How?

It depends on what we're up against.

He put thirty miles between them and the city before stopping at a shopping center.

"Just pick up a few things," he said. "You can use my toothpaste."

"I'm very particular about toothpaste. What brand?"

When he told her, she laughed. "I guess we were on the same wavelength there."

He knew she was trying for a light tone as she exited the car. He hesitated for a moment, then climbed out.

She looked at him.

"I don't want to leave you alone."

He pushed the shopping cart while she made some quick selections of T-shirts and jeans, then headed for the health section, where she picked up deodorant and moisturizer.

In some ways, it was such an ordinary domestic shopping trip. A man and his girlfriend getting a few things for a weekend getaway.

When she glanced at him, he knew she'd caught the thought.

But it's something I never expected to share.

Yes, she answered.

When she pulled out her credit card at the cash register, he shook his head.

"I'd better pay cash."

Right. I wasn't thinking.

I can use the money I took from baldy.

She laughed. *Perfect. And your gambling winnings.*

Yeah, there's that.

They finished up quickly, then headed for the town she'd mentioned. On the outskirts, she pointed to a bed-and-breakfast called Morning Glory that advertised cottages.

"What about there?"

He slowed and looked at the place, knowing it appealed to her.

"How are we going to pay," she asked, "if we can't use a credit card?"

"I still have money from that thug. He had a lot of cash on him."

"Yes. Good."

"Stay in the car while I register."

When she gave him a questioning look, he explained, "I don't want us seen together, if possible."

When he stepped into the office, he saw a middle-aged woman sitting at the desk. Her name tag read Helen Marcos.

"Can I help you?" she asked.

"My wife and I have been traveling around the area, and we'd like a nice room. In a private cottage, if possible."

"Magnolia Cottage is one of my best. It's got a bedroom and a sitting room and a large bathroom with a separate tub and shower."

"That sounds perfect."

He took the key and went back to the car. "I have a room I think you'll like," he said, feeling the tightness in his chest.

They'd both heard the phrase "get a room." They both knew why they were getting this room.

The cottage was white clapboard, with green shutters and a couple of wicker rocking chairs on the porch.

"Nice," Stephanie murmured as she inspected the exterior.

They were careful not to touch each other as they gathered their things.

Craig unlocked the door, and they stepped into a sitting room furnished with antique chests and tables and what looked like a comfortable chair and couch.

"Let me check it out," he said, taking a quick look at the bedroom and then the large bathroom. He came back to the bedroom and drew the drapes over the window, darkening the room.

When he turned around, he saw Stephanie was standing a few feet away.

The mixture of anticipation and uncertainty on her face made his mouth go dry. He hoped his expression was more certain. He had longed for this kind of connection since he'd lost Sam. They'd grown up together and forged a bond as naturally as breathing. And now he felt even closer to Stephanie. It must have something to do with the clinic, but he didn't know what that was yet. He knew he and Stephanie were on the verge of something astonishing. If they dared to take the next step.

"Are you afraid of this?" he managed to ask.

"You know I am."

"You think it would be possible to walk away from each other now?"

The question brought a spurt of panic. "No."

He saw her swallow.

"I never made love with John Reynard," she said.

"Thank God," he heard himself say.

"I came up with excuses."

As she spoke, she took a step forward, and he did the same. They reached for each other, swaying as they clung together.

It's going to be okay, he said.

We don't know that.

Do you want to...stop?

I don't think we can. Not now.

He absorbed the truth of her silent words as he lowered his mouth to hers for a long, hungry kiss.

When they'd gotten close before, they'd picked up thoughts from the other's past. Now there was nothing between them but this moment in time.

They were alone with each other. And this time nothing was going to stop them. And yet they both understood that they were taking a risk that neither of them fully understood.

Chapter Ten

Craig kissed her again, his hands moving over her back, down to her hips, pressing her middle to his erection, knowing they were about to change everything.

Everything already changed the first time we touched.

That was true, too.

His head was pounding, a counterpoint that he wished he could banish. But it seemed to come with the arousal.

Maybe this is like the first time a woman makes love—there's pain, she suggested.

Not a headache. That's a different cliché. But we should go back to what you said first. What if we have to break through a barrier between us?

How?

He sent her a very graphic picture. When she moved her body against his, he knew they were on the same wavelength.

He slipped his hands under the edge of her knit top, sighing as he stroked the soft skin of her back.

Then he reached up to unhook her bra so that he could slide his hands to her front and cup her breasts, gliding his thumbs across the hardened crests.

"Oh."

He bent to kiss her again, his goal to make her so hot that she couldn't think about anything besides what they were doing together. Maybe that was the way to wipe out the pain building inside his skull.

He knew she'd captured that thought when she slid her hand down the front of his body, cupping his erection, rocking her palm against him.

Not too much of that. I want this to last.

She raised her hands, doing what he had done, slipping her fingers under his T-shirt so that she could stroke his back before pushing the fabric up.

He stepped away from her and pulled the shirt over his head.

By the time he'd tossed the shirt away, he saw that she was standing in front of him naked to the waist.

He stared at her in the dim light coming through the crack at the edge of the curtains. "You are so beautiful."

She grinned. "Your chest isn't bad, either."

He crossed to the bathroom, turning on the light and leaving the door a little ajar. When he looked back to her, he saw that she had turned down the covers and was reaching for the button at the top of her slacks.

"Let me."

She went still as he crossed to her, worked the button, then slowly lowered the zipper so that he could shuck her pants down her legs, taking her panties with them.

He felt so much. Too much. Sexual arousal, the thoughts leaping toward him—and the pounding in his head that might wipe out everything else.

He strove to put that worry out of his mind. It wouldn't happen if they did this right.

Which was what, exactly?

As he caressed her, he moved his lips against hers, stroking then nibbling with his teeth. He knew the exact amount of pressure that would bring her pleasure instead of pain, because he felt her reactions as well as his own.

She was busy, too, removing his pants and briefs.

Finally they were naked in each other's arms, and his need for her threatened to overwhelm him.

If he didn't make love with her...

He couldn't finish the thought because he knew that neither one of them could stop. If he pulled away from her now, his brain would explode. And if he didn't pull away, the same thing might happen.

She understood all that, and he sensed her fear. But they clung together, never breaking the contact as they staggered to the bed and fell onto the mattress. He rolled toward her, gathering her close, his body rocking against hers, both of them gasping at the sensation of skin against skin.

They were both trembling, coping with more than it seemed possible to bear. His head throbbed, and he knew that he might stroke out from the intensity.

He heard her gasp. Not just the sound, but in his mind—generated by the same pain he felt.

But he couldn't let her go.

Maybe that was the key to survival. The courage to see this through—no matter where it led.

Remembering his vow to arouse her to fever pitch, he slid his hand down her body again, dipping into the folds high up between her legs. She was wet and molten for him, and he didn't have to ask if she was ready to take the final step. He knew.

And she didn't have to use her hand to guide him into her. They simply did it, moving from separate individuals to one being in a smooth, sure motion.

He was inside her. Or was she inside him? He didn't know anymore where he ended and she began. He only knew that every sense was tuned to her. Every thought. And she to him.

One of them began to move. No, it was both of them, because the pressure in their brains was too great and the only way to relieve it was through sexual climax.

That didn't make sense. Yet he thought it was true, at least with the part of his mind that could still function coherently.

Or was it simply instinct that had him grasping for orgasm and bringing her along with him, because if it didn't end soon, he knew he would die.

He couldn't make absolute sense of that, but he was far beyond trying to understand what was happening. He was captive to the fiery sensations—his and hers—that were rushing them toward ecstasy…or death.

He couldn't have stopped now if the door had burst open and men with guns had come charging in, firing at point-blank range.

He clung to Stephanie and she to him. Not just with his hands but with his mind. He had thought he was searching for remembered intimacy. This was so much more that he was at a loss to comprehend it. Yet as he hovered on the edge of a blinding explosion inside his brain, he wasn't sure he would survive.

Only the woman who held him in her arms saved him from destruction.

And because every barrier between them had vanished, he knew it was the same for her. They would die together—or pull each other into a new life.

They crashed through an invisible barrier that separated them from everything they had always known. Climax shook them, blinding them to everything but what they had forged. They clung tightly to each other as they came down to earth, each of them panting, each of them marveling at what they had done together.

In that moment, there was nothing he could hide from

her. Nothing she could hide from him. He didn't even try, just drifted on the perfect oneness of their shared consciousness.

Since his brother's death, he had felt cut off from humanity. This woman had filled the empty void within himself. More than filled it. She had given him a perfect union that he never could have imagined.

I always felt alone, she whispered in his mind. *Not now.*

He held her and stroked her, so grateful that she was in his arms.

But I still don't understand it, she silently added.

I thought I did. This is more than I ever imagined, he answered.

She clasped his hand and held on tight. *Making love gave us everything we wanted, but it could have killed us. If...*

If we had a failure of nerve.

You knew what we could gain.

I only thought I knew.

Neither one of us was going to give up.

Rolling to his side, he took her with him, feeling more peaceful than he had since the terrible day Sam had died.

Emotionally exhausted, he felt sleep wafting over him and tried to fight it off.

Yes, I don't want to lose a moment of this, she whispered in his mind.

I'll be here when you wake up. I'll always be here, he answered. But for the moment, it was impossible not to drift off after the energy they had expended.

BACK IN NEW ORLEANS, a woman named Rachel Harper went very still. She was alone in her shop in the French Quarter where she did tarot-card readings and sold psychic paraphernalia. Once she had been alone and isolated, and she'd used her ability with the cards to connect with people on a level that would have been impossible otherwise. But last year she had met a man who had changed her life. Jake Harper.

The two of them had bonded in a way she had never dared imagine. And being with him had changed her life in ways she was still trying to understand.

As she sat alone in her darkened reading room, a burst of mental energy came to her from miles away. It startled her, and she knew she wouldn't be alone here for long. Only a few minutes passed before the door to her shop burst open, and her husband, Jake, rushed in, out of breath from running.

He'd been in his office at one of the restaurants he owned in the city.

Something happened. Are you all right? he asked.

Yes.

Are we in danger?

I don't know, she answered honestly.

Jake crossed to her side, reaching for her hand and folding her fingers around his. For long moments, neither of them moved or spoke, although speech was no longer necessary for the two of them to communicate.

You sensed another couple bonding, he finally said.

I think so.

Are they going to attack us?

Someone who didn't know their history might have thought the question paranoid, but the first couple like them that they'd encountered, Tanya and Mickey, had tried to kill them. The fight for their lives had made them cautious.

They were thinking the same thing now.

We have to wait and see what happens.

Are they in trouble?

Probably.

Does that mean we *have a new enemy? I don't mean them. I mean...someone connected with the Solomon Clinic.*

I guess we'll find out.

SOMETIME DURING THE NIGHT, Stephanie woke. Beside her, so did Craig.

He eased far enough away to switch on the bedside lamp, and they both blinked in the sudden glow.

When he raised himself on his elbow and smiled down at her, she felt her own smile starting with her mouth and spreading through her whole body.

"Would you have believed that could happen—if anyone had told you?"

"No."

"We've found something nobody else has."

"Maybe somebody," she answered.

"Who?"

"You think there's nobody like us? I mean, you and Sam had it."

"Close. But not exactly."

"Before we had to leave my dad's house, we were talking about the Solomon Clinic. About maybe it having something to do with..." She raised one shoulder. "I don't know how to put it, exactly. With children who had special abilities. Maybe we should look up the place."

"Nice that I was able to get my computer from the bed-and-breakfast."

As he went to retrieve his laptop, she admired his broad shoulders and tight butt.

I heard that.

She flushed. *I guess there are some disadvantages to... being so...open to each other.*

Sam and I used to practice closing off our minds from each other. We could try that.

And that other thing—that you didn't mention.

He went still, then turned around. *You mean putting thoughts into people's minds.*

Yes, that. Why didn't you say something about it?

Even as she asked the question, she knew that he'd considered it a questionable skill. Like stealing.

I understand, she answered. *But it might come in handy when someone is trying to kidnap you—or kill you.*

Yeah.

When he returned with the laptop, she had an opportunity to admire him from the front. And although she did her best to keep her thoughts to herself, she knew he'd picked them up again.

As he slipped into bed beside her, she asked, "How *do* you keep from having everything in your mind like an open book?"

"You build a wall."

"Like how?"

"With Sam, I used to picture a wall made out of metal plates. Let me show you."

She saw the concentration on his face as he made the wall. Reaching for his hand, she held on tight as she tried to get into his mind and came up against the barrier. Maybe there was a way around it, but she didn't find it as she searched.

You try it, he suggested.

She tried to do the same thing he had done, make a wall that would block out her thoughts. It was easy to picture the wall but not so easy to keep it in place.

I'd spend a lot of energy keeping it intact, she said, struggling with a sense of defeat.

Keep practicing, and you'll get better. I hadn't done it in years, and it came back to me.

She built fortresses in her head while he booted up his computer.

"You think there's anything on the web after all these years?"

"We'll find out."

She moved beside him where she could see the screen, pulling the sheet up over her breasts.

He glanced at her and grinned. "I've seen them."

She flushed. "I know, but I'm not as casual about walking around naked as you are."

She knew from his thoughts that he planned to desensitize her—in the shower.

I should practice that wall thing, he answered.

She smiled and moved her shoulder against his. It would have been impossible for her to imagine this wonderful closeness with anyone. But Craig had changed her world.

Mine, too. When the computer finished its start-up routine, he went to Google, looking for information about the Solomon Clinic. At first they found nothing. Then he added Houma, and a startling newspaper entry came up.

"The explosion at a research laboratory owned by Dr. Douglas Solomon is under investigation. The facility was being used by Dr. Solomon for medical research. His body was found in the wreckage of the lab, along with Violet Goodell, who was the head nurse at the doctor's former fertility clinic and also a close personal friend. She was active in charity work in Houma. Another body found in the wreckage was that of William Wellington, former head of the Howell Institute, a Washington think tank. According to anonymous sources in Houma, Wellington may have had a financial interest in the Solomon fertility clinic, but it is not known why he was at the research facility when it exploded.

The Solomon Clinic was in operation until the early nineties, when it burned to the ground in a fire that was believed to be the result of arson. There were no casualties.

Dr. Solomon was a native of Houma. His clinic drew patients from all over the U.S., but principally from Louisiana and neighboring states, and was instrumental in helping over two hundred women conceive. Although the clinic was known for charging high fees to wealthy clients, it also took less-well-off patients at greatly reduced fees. After the facility burned down, the doctor maintained a low profile, but his research facility is believed to have developed vaccines for several nationally prominent drug companies."

Stephanie looked at Craig. "That article is interesting, as much for what it doesn't say as for what it does."

"Yeah."

Craig went back to the search panel and looked up the doctor's biography. He was a Yale graduate who had gone on to Harvard Medical School, then returned to his hometown to open his fertility clinic.

"I guess he was pretty smart," Stephanie murmured. "I'd like to see his records from the fertility clinic, but they probably burned."

"That may be the reason for the earlier fire—to get rid of the records."

"Why?"

"It sounds like he was doing more than fertility treatments." She looked from the computer screen to Craig. "We should go there."

"Not until our skills are more solid."

"Why?"

"I'm thinking we're going to need them to defend our-selves."

Stephanie shuddered, and she knew Craig had picked up on her thoughts as she felt him stroke his hand down her arm.

We just found each other—why can't whoever it is just leave us alone?

Because there's something important about the children from the clinic. And someone's interested in what it is.

When Stephanie jolted, Craig didn't have to ask what had leaped into her mind.

We both forgot we got that phone number.

You want to call it? He asked.

She considered the question. *I don't think that's going to get us any information. And we'd just be revealing some-thing about us.*

Yeah. Forget calling.

Chapter Eleven

Harold Goddard slapped his fist against his left palm, but the physical gesture did nothing to relieve his anger.

He was used to working with professionals, and now he was finding out the pitfalls of relying on local talent.

The men he'd hired had had Stephanie Swift and Craig Branson in custody—and the incompetent asses had let the couple get away.

They'd compounded the mistake by waiting a couple of hours before reporting their failure.

"Tell me again what happened," he said to Wayne Channing, the bald-headed man who had been recommended to him as the best there was if you needed an undercover job done in the Big Easy.

"Like you said, we looked for them at her father's place and found them there. They were climbing out an upstairs window, and they dropped right into our laps. We took them to the van, with our holding her at gunpoint and his cooperating so she wouldn't get hurt. We loaded them in the van and taped their hands and feet."

"And then what?"

"Something happened. We was in the middle of traffic, and they got loose and got out the back door."

"How did they get loose?"

"We don't know."

"Didn't you restrain them securely?"

"We thought we did."

"You thought?" Harold said in a calm voice when he wanted to scream.

"Somehow they got away."

"Did you look at the tape?"

"No."

"Bring me the tape. Well, leave it in a plastic bag next to the Dumpster at that shopping center where I wanted you to bring them."

There was a moment's hesitation before Channing said, "Yes, sir."

"And how did they get the better of you at the B and B?" Harold asked.

"They spotted us, then made a tricky move. She acted like she didn't see me, and he snuck up behind and brained me."

Harold thought for a few minutes. He could yell at this guy. He could bring him in and kill him. But that would be counterproductive because he'd just have to find someone else to do the work.

"After you drop off the tape, I want you to go to Houma, Louisiana, and stake out a building in the business district." He gave the address. "I expect they are going to show up there."

He thought about what had apparently happened in the van and what he thought might be going on with the children who had been born as a result of their mothers' treatments at the Solomon Clinic.

"When you catch them, make sure you separate them. I don't want them touching each other. Understood?"

"Yes, sir," Channing answered.

WE HAVE TO STRENGTHEN *our powers,* Craig said when they woke up the next morning, too late for breakfast.

How?

When Stephanie caught the suggestion forming in Craig's mind, she gave him a doubtful look.

You don't think that will be effective? Even if we've never done it before? he asked.

Before she could make any decisions on her own, he had her out of the bed and into the bathroom. He turned on the shower and let the water run hot before helping her into the tile enclosure where a rain shower sent a torrent down on her.

The heated water turned her skin slick and sensitive, and her whole body tightened as he pulled her close.

For long moments, he simply held her, the two of them standing together under the pounding spray.

From behind her, he began to run soap-slick hands over her back and shoulders. As they glided with a total absence of resistance, they sent heat vibrating through her body.

He turned her in his arms and brought his mouth to hers for a heated kiss while he angled her upper body away from his so that he could stroke his hands over her breasts, turning her nipples into taut peaks of sensation.

She squeezed her eyes closed, focused only on Craig Branson and the sensations he was creating—and the thoughts pouring off him as he told her how much it meant to him to have found her, how much he wanted her, how much he loved her.

Love.

The word stunned her. She had never expected to love anyone. She hadn't even loved her parents, she silently acknowledged, which was probably why she had let her father persuade her to marry the wrong man.

But everything had changed.

I love you, she answered him, sure it was true, even though she had known him such a short time. But what had happened between them had changed her life. Had changed everything.

He lowered his mouth to hers for a long, hungry kiss as his hand stroked down the length of her bare back, sending heat shooting through her as he caressed her bare bottom.

As his hands slid over her, wet heat pooled between her legs. She knew he felt it, felt it in his own body. And she felt the fullness of his erection, felt his need to join with her.

The need built, pulsing through her and through him in time to the wild beating of their hearts.

And she knew what he wanted her to do. Following his lead, she slicked her hand with soap and wrapped her fingers around his jutting erection, starting with a teasing stroke that drew a strangled breath from him. When she closed her fingers tightly around him, the breath turned into a moan.

Looking down, she grinned at the effect she had created. He'd been fully aroused when she'd started. Now he was impossibly hard.

She caught what he had in mind, and tried to do what he'd suggested before.

And suddenly the water stopped, leaving them standing in the shower, dripping.

You did that.

Yeah. And now I get my reward.

Leaning back against the side of the shower, he lifted her into his arms. She cried out as he filled her, holding her against himself as he turned on the water again with his mind so that it pounded down on them once more. His movement was restricted by his braced hips. But as he held her, she moved her body, the friction taking them to a high peak where the air was almost too thin to breathe.

She loved the intensity on his face—in his mind—as she quickened the pace.

His exclamation made her raise her head as she stared at the water pouring down on them. She had stopped thinking about the water, but now it was pulsing in time to the movements of her body.

She drove them to a sharp, all-encompassing climax that radiated to every part of her body while the shower seemed to explode in a cascade of water.

She felt Craig follow her into ecstasy, and as they came back to themselves, the shower settled down to a normal flow.

She heard Craig's silent laugh. *That last part was...*

Unexpected, she finished as she collapsed against him and he lowered her to her feet.

Proof we can do more with our minds than we thought.

I don't believe we can count on sexual arousal every time we need to generate psychic power, she answered.

He reached for a towel and trapped it around her shoulders, then began to dry her off.

As he did, she caught the thought in his mind.

You're full of ideas, she answered.

You don't think we should try it?

Is it ethical?

We're not going to harm anyone. We're just going to have a practice session.

THEY GOT DRESSED, left the room and stopped at the office to ask for lunch recommendations.

Mrs. Marcos suggested several restaurants, and they decided on a place with a deck along the bayou and an extensive seafood menu.

On the way over, they discussed Craig's plan.

The restaurant was pleasantly decorated with rough-hewn wood on the walls and old-time photographs from the twenties and thirties. The dining room was about half-full, with plenty of tables available both inside and out.

They walked in and stood together waiting for the hostess to return to the podium. She was a young woman with curly blond hair and a bright smile.

"We'd like a table," Craig said without volunteering any other information. But silently he was asking to sit out on the deck—along the railing.

"I have a lovely spot on the deck along the railing," the hostess said.

Craig gave Stephanie a satisfied look. "That would be great," he said to the hostess.

They followed her outside, to the only prime spot left at the edge of the deck.

"Your server is Julian, and he will be right with you," the woman said before she left.

"That went well," Craig said when they were alone.

"It doesn't prove anything. She could have just decided to give us this spot."

He shrugged. "Okay, we'll see what we can get the server to do."

A dark-haired young man wearing a black T-shirt and black pants approached the table carrying a pitcher of water.

"Hi, I'm Julian, and I'll be your server this evening."

They'd silently agreed that Craig would get him not to pour the water and ask if they wanted tea instead.

As he lifted the pitcher, she fed Craig energy.

Julian's hand shook for a moment, and he lowered the pitcher, a strange expression on his face.

"Uh, I was wondering, would you prefer iced tea?" he asked.

"Why, yes, we would," Craig answered.

"Sweetened?" he asked.

"Correct again."

"I'll be right back with your tea."

When the young man had departed, Craig wiggled his eyebrows suggestively at Stephanie.

She laughed. "Okay, that was pretty good. Maybe we can work up a stage act."

"Yeah, it *was* good, and you can't argue that he was pushing tea instead of water."

She nodded and opened the menu, scanning the entries. "Now what?"

"Get him to suggest that we try the popcorn shrimp?"

"Too easy. He's probably already thinking about them."

CRAIG RAN HIS FINGER down the menu. "Get him to sell us the fried okra."

"Have you ever tasted it?"

"No."

"It's an acquired taste. Let's try something else."

He turned back to the menu. "Okay, buffalo wings."

When the server returned and set down their glasses of tea, he asked, "Can I get you started with an appetizer?"

"What's good?"

Again Stephanie let Craig make the silent suggestion to the man while she added her power to his mental push.

"I think you'll love the buffalo wings," Julian said.

"Excellent," Craig answered. "Bring us an order."

He slid his foot along the deck boards and rested his shoe against Stephanie's. "Score another one for us."

Making food selections isn't that hard. Do you think we could have made those thugs who kidnapped us put down their guns?

Not then. Maybe now, Craig answered.

You'd bet your life on that?

No. That's why we're practicing.

We're just playing games, she shot back.

That's all we can do—unless you want to get some-one in town to rob a bank. It's got to be stuff that's within bounds of the law.

I don't think you're going to get that guy to jump into the bayou. And I don't want to suggest something that would get him fired—like tossing the buffalo wings over the rail-ing. What if we see if we can get him to deliver them to the wrong table?

Okay.

They relaxed at their table, sipping their iced tea. When Stephanie saw the waiter come back with the wings, she sent Craig a silent message. *He's here.*

Craig let her direct the next part, but she felt him lend-ing energy. She told the guy to deliver the appetizer to the table in back of them, and she saw his face take on a con-fused look. He stopped for a second, then walked past them to the next table.

Behind her she heard the couple telling Julian that they hadn't ordered the wings. In fact, they were waiting for their dessert.

He did a quick about-face and came back to Craig and Stephanie, his cheeks flushed.

"Sorry about that. I don't know how I got mixed up."

"Don't worry about it," Craig said.

We have to stop playing with him, Stephanie said when he'd left the food and departed.

Yeah, poor guy.

They ate the wings and ordered shrimp étouffée and grilled snapper, which they shared before returning to their cottage for some more intimate practice sessions.

Worn-out, they fell asleep, but the events of the past few days had taken their toll.

JOHN REYNARD PICKED UP the phone. The police detective on the other end of the line said, "I have some information for you." The caller was the guy he'd sent over to the dress shop earlier who took substantial amounts of money under the table to keep Reynard informed on police-department business.

"Go ahead."

"I have a fingerprint report on the man who called himself Craig Brady."

"That's not his name?"

"He's Craig Branson. He's a private detective out of the Washington, D.C., area."

"What the hell is he doing here?"

"I'm working on that. He made an inquiry about a body that turned up in the bayou. A guy named Arthur Polaski."

John felt a frisson go through him. How did Branson know about *that?*

"You think Branson is in New Orleans investigating Polaski's death?"

"Or what he did before he was killed."

"Yeah, thanks for the heads-up."

The cop hesitated. "I think one of the other guys in the department gave Branson the heads-up about Polaski."

"Why?"

"Apparently Branson made it his business to keep in touch."

Oh, great, John thought. But then he supposed if you had a police department full of informants, you couldn't control who was giving out information to whom.

"You need anything else?" his contact asked.

"Can you find out if Branson has used his credit card recently? Maybe I can get a line on where he went."

"Okay. Do you want him arrested?"

"For what?"

"He's down here using an assumed name. We could have him brought in for questioning."

"Yeah. That might be good. If you can find him."

"There could be an accident while he's in custody."

"Even better."

STEPHANIE KNEW she was dreaming, but there was nothing she could do about it and no way she could stop the course of events her mind had conjured up.

The dream started at her father's house. She and Craig climbed out the window and down to the ground. Then she rounded the corner and ran into the two thugs with the guns. Only this time was different. This time she was alone.

They hustled her to the van, and she kept crying out in her mind, crying out for Craig, but he simply wasn't there. She was totally alone. The way she had been all her life. Only now she knew what it was like to be bonded with her soul mate. But he wasn't there. He had vanished. And she couldn't go on alone. Not after what she'd found with him.

The two thugs were there, but they weren't her only captors. John Reynard stood over them, telling them to tape her hands and feet. He was telling them to take her away, to a place where Craig could never find her.

His eyes met hers, and she felt ice forming in her chest and throat.

"You betrayed me with that man."

"No," she lied.

"You belong to me," he said. "I'll take you back, but only if you promise never to see that other guy again."

Her mouth worked, but no words came out. How could she make that promise? How could she say she would never see Craig again? That would be as good as death.

Chapter Twelve

In the dream, the two thugs were holding her down in the back of the van, and she struggled against them, knowing that if they drove away with her, she was dead. Desperate to escape, she kicked out with her foot, making one of them gasp.

Good.

Someone was calling her name, and it didn't sound like either of the men who had taken her captive, or like John.

"Stephanie. For Lord's sake, Stephanie."

She heard the words in her ears—and in her mind. And they finally penetrated through the dream.

It was Craig. He was here, calling her, holding her.

Her eyes blinked open, and she stared up at him, catching his relief.

Stephanie.

Craig, she answered. *I was so scared. I was dreaming those men had me, and John was there.*

I know. I caught the edge of the dream as you started to wake up.

I thought I'd lost you.

You'll never lose me.

She sighed deeply as she held on to him, overwhelmed with gratitude that he was here—with her. Yet she knew he couldn't make the promise to be with her always. He could be yanked away from her, the way his brother had been yanked away from him.

No. I promise.

Despite his reassurance, her thoughts were racing. *Something awful is going to happen. We have to get away before it does. Can't we leave Louisiana? Go somewhere nobody knows us?*

She caught his reluctance to consider the desperate suggestion. *I understand why you want to run, but we won't really be safe until we find out who's after us.*

How do we do it?

The answer must be in Houma.

She shuddered. *I don't want to go there.*

I know. He gathered her closer, running his hands up and down her back, combing his fingers through her hair, stroking his lips against her cheek.

She relaxed into his embrace, so grateful to have him.

The feeling's mutual, he murmured in her mind.

He rocked her in his arms, and when he began to make love to her, she brought her face up for a long, heated kiss.

JOHN REYNARD RANG the elder Swift's doorbell and waited, impatiently tapping his foot on the floorboards of the wide front porch.

It was early in the morning, earlier than he liked to be making a business call, but he had spent a restless night worrying about Stephanie. She'd disappeared, and he had to find her.

He'd gotten a call back on the Craig Branson credit card. It hadn't been used, which meant that the guy was being careful about revealing where he was.

The last John knew, Stephanie was with him, and he meant to find her. And get her away from the guy.

Was she a prisoner? Or had she willingly gone with the

bastard? And what had Branson told her to get her to go along with whatever the bastard had in mind? Had he told her about the body of Arthur Polaski?

But why would he? Unless he was trying to turn her against her fiancé.

One thing John knew was that she'd left her car at home. Of course, there was no absolute proof that she was with Branson, but it was John's best guess.

In the middle of the night, he'd sent a message to a P.I. who worked in the D.C. area and started the guy checking into Branson's background, looking for something that would explain why the man had shown up to investigate a twenty-two-year-old murder. And why he was dragging Stephanie around.

When no one answered the door, he rang again.

"I'm coming," a voice called from inside.

The crackly old voice sounded like Henri Swift.

Half a minute later, a shadow appeared behind the lace curtain that covered the glass panel in the middle of the door. Finally the barrier was pulled open, and John and one of his men stepped inside.

Swift blinked at him. He was wearing an old burgundy satin dressing gown. His hair was mussed, and his cheeks were covered with gray stubble. Obviously his visitor had gotten him out of bed. "What are you doing here at this time in the morning?"

"Looking for my fiancée."

"She isn't here."

"Maybe not now. But was she?"

When Swift hesitated, John wanted to smack him upside the head. "Answer yes or no."

"I think she was here."

The answer elicited a curse. "Are you saying you don't

know for sure? Are you saying she came in and didn't speak to you?"

"I was out."

"Doing what?"

Swift's face tightened. "Getting supplies."

"Liquor?"

"I was running low."

John made a disparaging sound.

"I came home, and I thought she was in the house. But when I looked for her, she'd snuck out. If she was here at all."

"What makes you think she was here?"

Swift shifted his weight from one foot to the other. "I don't appreciate your barging in on me like this."

"Oh, you don't? Well, you don't have much choice."

"We have an agreement."

"That's right, and I don't know where the hell to find your daughter. If she was here, I want to know why and where she went."

"All right. I heard someone upstairs, but nobody was there. When I investigated, I saw that the bedspread in her mother's room was mussed."

John felt a wave of anger sweep over him. She hadn't made love with him, but had she come here to do the deed with Branson? "You mean she was on the bed with someone?"

"I don't think so. I think she took a bunch of boxes out of the closet and put them on the bed."

"You're quite the detective."

"It's my best guess."

"Show me the bedroom." He turned to the bodyguard he'd brought along. "Wait here."

"Yes sir."

John was already barreling up the stairs, then had to wait for the old man to come huffing after him.

He led the way down the hall to a bedroom that looked as if it hadn't been touched in years.

"What boxes? Why?"

Swift opened the closet and pointed to the top shelf. "That's stuff my wife kept around. Stuff I couldn't throw out."

"And why do you think Stephanie was into it?"

"The boxes aren't piled up exactly the way they were."

"I mean, what was she looking for?"

"I don't know."

John marched to the closet and pulled the boxes down. He could see folders and piles of old papers. Photographs and schoolwork from when Stephanie had been little. He wasn't interested in the sentimental crap, but he looked at the pictures anyway, trying to find something that would give him a clue.

There were photos of the family when Stephanie was little. He hoped he wasn't going to find that guy Branson's smiling face.

That thought gave him pause. She didn't know him from her past, did she?

He looked up, seeing Swift watching him.

"Get me some coffee. No cream. No sugar."

He could see the man wanted to say he wasn't John Reynard's servant, but he kept his mouth shut and shuffled out of the room. John could hear him rattling around downstairs, then a few minutes later Swift brought a mug of coffee. At least it was a strong New Orleans brew laced with chicory. John sipped while he looked through folders, wondering if anything would strike him. And wondering why he was bothering. Maybe because if he couldn't have Stephanie with him, he could at least paw through her past.

The notion made him snort. John Reynard didn't settle for less than he was due. But in this case, he'd have to settle until he could change the equation.

He came across some forms and instructions from a place called the Solomon Clinic in Houma. Apparently it was a fertility clinic. And it looked as if Stephanie's mother had gone there for treatments before she was born. That was interesting. Did it mean that Stephanie would have trouble conceiving children? He hadn't considered that when he'd decided he had to marry her because it certainly hadn't been his main reason for wanting to keep her close. Kids would be good, though, because it was a way to keep hold of her. If she was worried about losing custody of her children, she wouldn't be quick to leave her husband. But that was all in the future. It didn't give him a clue to where she was now. He put the folder back into the box and kept looking for information he could use.

"Do you have a second home?" he asked Swift.

"Yes."

"Where?"

He gave the location.

That might be a possibility.

When his cell phone rang, he looked at the number with annoyance, displeased to be interrupted in the middle of his search.

Then he recognized the area code and knew it was the guy in D.C. he'd hired to dig up stuff on Craig Branson. Maybe he'd found something that would be more useful than these piles of old papers and pictures.

He got up, walked into the hall and answered the phone.

"Mr. Reynard?" the detective said.

"Yeah."

"I've been digging into Branson's past."

"Have you found any dirt?"

"Not anything illegal that he's done, but he was involved in an incident a number of years ago."

John felt his heart leap. Was this something he could use?

"What?" he demanded.

"He and his family were eating dinner in a restaurant when a mob boss named Jackie Montana was gunned down."

John felt the hairs on his arms prickle.

The man continued, "The guy and two of his bodyguards went down. It turns out Branson's twin brother, Sam, was collateral damage."

An exclamation of disbelief sprang to John's lips. "You mean at a place called Venario's?" he managed to ask.

"You know about it?"

"It made the news," John answered. He'd ordered that mob hit because Jackie Montana had been trying to muscle in on John's New Orleans operation. John had known that there were some civilians hit, but he'd never paid attention to the names of the victims. That hadn't been his concern.

"You're sure about that?" he asked now.

"Yes."

John's head was buzzing, but something the man was saying penetrated the swirling thoughts in his brain.

"What did you say?" he asked.

"Which part?"

"About the clinic."

"Okay. Yeah. After Sam died, the mother tried to get in touch with a place called the Solomon Clinic. Down your way, in Houma."

"Okay. Thanks. You have the address."

"I have the old address, but the place burned down."

They talked for a few more minutes before John hung up.

"Thanks for your help," he said to Swift.

"I didn't do much."

"You noticed."

When he started out of the room, the older man called out, "Hey, what about all that stuff on the bed?"

"I'm sure you can put it away."

He knew Swift was angry, which pleased him.

Outside he turned to his man. "You and Marv are going down to Houma."

"For what?"

"Stephanie and that bozo she's with might show up there."

"Like where, exactly?"

"There was a clinic down there they might want to check out. I'll get you the address."

"WE CAN LEAVE our things here and drive over to Houma," Craig said.

"And do what, exactly?"

"We could start with the archives at the local papers, or we could try something else."

When she asked for details, he said, "I'll tell you about it on the way over."

They walked to the main house, where Mrs. Marcos was in the dining room.

"I hope you slept well," she said brightly.

"Yes, of course," Stephanie answered. "The cottage is charming."

"You can sit anywhere you like. Breakfast is served buffet-style."

They took a table by the window, then helped themselves to the buffet on the sideboard, indulging in the coffee cake and muffins that Mrs. Marcos had set out—along with her spinach quiche and strong Louisiana coffee.

"I didn't see you at breakfast yesterday. Are you enjoying your stay?" the B and B owner asked as they were finishing their breakfast.

"It's perfect," Stephanie answered.

"And we enjoyed your accommodations so much that we're hoping to keep our room for another night," Craig added.

"That would be fine. Where are you off to today?"

"We thought we'd drive over to Houma."

"It's a lovely little town."

"Didn't I read about some kind of explosion there?" Craig asked.

Mrs. Marcos's expression clouded. "Yes. At an underground research lab," she said, then pressed her lips together, indicating that she didn't want to continue the subject.

What do you mean by "underground"? Craig asked.

"Nobody in town knew Dr. Solomon was still doing research." The woman stopped, looking confused. "Well, I guess some people did know. Like his nurse, Mrs. Goodell. She worked for him at the old clinic…." Her voice trailed off. "I don't know why I'm prattling on like this. I have things to do in the kitchen."

"You're just being friendly," Stephanie said in a pleasant voice when her heart was pounding. She added her psychic power as she let Craig direct the message he sent the B and B owner.

If you know anything more about the Solomon Clinic or Dr. Solomon, tell it to us now. He repeated the suggestion, waiting tensely for what she would decide.

The outcome wasn't a sure thing. Stephanie could see the woman going through a debate in her mind, and she felt Craig pushing the idea.

"So who was this Dr. Solomon?" Stephanie asked.

"Thirty years ago, he had a fertility clinic," she said

as though she didn't really want to speak the words. "My friend Darla Dubour went to him, and she was so appreciative when she got pregnant. She had a little boy. David."

"It's always nice when medical treatment works out," Stephanie said brightly. She caught a stray thought from Craig and asked, "Where is her son now?"

The woman's eyes clouded. "He died."

Stephanie sucked in a startled breath. "What happened to him?"

"I should stop talking about this."

"I'm sorry. I don't know how we got on the subject. I guess we were just looking for information about Houma so we could plan our day."

"You can get that from the chamber of commerce or the town hall."

"Yes, thanks," Stephanie said, but the other woman was already bustling toward the dining-room entrance, where another couple was waiting to be seated.

I guess we hit some kind of nerve, Stephanie said to Craig when they were alone again.

Yeah. There must have been some blowback from the Solomon Clinic.

Or it's because that woman's son died.

I think we should go see her.

You think she'll talk to us? Stephanie asked.

Maybe we can use the same method, Craig answered.

I hate doing that to a grieving mother.

I don't love it, either, but if it saves our lives, I'm willing to try it.

She winced.

They went back to their room, where they used the computer to look up Darla Dubour in Houma, Louisiana, and found that she lived in a small community outside of town.

"Should we call her?" Stephanie asked.

"I think it's better if we just go over unannounced."

They were in the car and on their way a few minutes after they'd looked up the location.

Stephanie felt a chill go through her.

Craig reached to cover her hand with his. "You're thinking we're going to find out something bad about ourselves when we talk to that woman?"

"Yes."

WAYNE CHANNING and his partner, Buck Arnot, Harold Goddard's men, had arrived in Houma the evening before.

Because they'd been ordered to stake out the location where the Solomon Clinic had been located, they had spent an uncomfortable night in their car in a grocery-store parking lot where they could see the target location.

"Got to pee," Wayne said as he moved restlessly in his seat.

"There's a gas station a couple blocks down."

"But we're supposed to keep the building in sight."

Channing sighed. "This is a real long shot."

"But we got our orders."

"Okay, I'll drive down to the gas station and do my thing. You stay here and watch the building."

"And get arrested for loitering."

"Walk up the sidewalk and back again, like you're out for your morning constitutional."

"Yeah, right. Come back with coffee and doughnuts."

"What flavor?"

"Surprise me." Buck climbed out and watched his partner drive off. When he was out of sight, he ducked around by the Dumpsters. He didn't need a smelly gas station to relieve himself. Then he started down the block, looking in shop windows.

When he got to the cross street, he turned and walked back, then did it again.

He was going to call Wayne on his cell and ask if he'd fallen into the gas-station toilet when he saw something interesting.

A car turned in at the grocery-store parking lot where he and his partner had spent the night. As he watched, two tough-looking men got out and stretched, as if they'd just finished a long drive.

Their gazes were fixed on the building that he and Wayne had been watching.

When he saw his partner coming back, he flagged him down and climbed back into the car.

"I can go into that parking lot and we can switch. You can drive to the gas station, and I'll wait here."

"I already done it out by the Dumpsters."

Wayne made a disgusted sound. "Didn't your mama teach you better?"

Ignoring the comment, Buck said, "Keep on drivin' past that parking lot."

The urgency in his voice made Wayne glance toward the lot, then speed up.

"Two tough-looking guys," he said.

"Yeah. I'm thinkin' they might have the same assignment we do."

"Why?"

He shrugged. "Must be a lot of interest in Swift and Branson."

"So what are we gonna do?"

"Call the guy who hired us and ask for instructions."

"He's probably still sleeping.'

Buck's voice took on a nasty tone as he turned toward his partner. "Well, we got reason to wake him up."

Chapter Thirteen

"I thought we'd take a look around town before we talk to Mrs. Dubour's," Craig said as he pulled out of the driveway of the B and B.

Stephanie closed her hand around his arm.

"Don't go there."

His gaze shot to her, then back to the road as he tuned in to her thoughts.

"You think it's dangerous to go into Houma," he said aloud, considering the implication of her words.

"Yes."

He silently debated her assessment. "You think the men who kidnapped us might be looking for us there."

"Yes."

"Which would mean they know something about the Solomon Clinic."

She nodded.

"Okay, we can go straight to Darla Dubour's."

"How are we going to approach her?"

"I think honesty is best. We tell her that we found out we were born as a result of treatments our mothers received at the Solomon Clinic and came to Houma to see if we could find out more about the clinic. We were talking to Mrs. Marcos, and she told us about David, and we'd like some more information, if she can give it to us."

"And if she doesn't want to talk to us?"

"We try our new technique."

RACHEL HARPER SHUFFLED a deck of tarot cards and laid one of them on the table.

Her husband, Jake, took in the worried expression on her face.

"It's the Hierophant, isn't it?" he said.

"Yes. He's the archetype of the spiritual world. The card can refer to a person who holds forbidden or secret knowledge."

"Which means what, in this case?"

She sighed. "You know how relieved we were when Solomon and Wellington were killed."

Jake nodded.

"Suppose there's someone else who knows about the children from the Solomon Clinic?"

"And he's trying something similar to what Wellington was doing?"

She clenched and unclenched her fists. "Yes."

"Which means we should stay away from him."

"Or it means we need to reach out to that other couple. Unless they turn out to be our enemies."

"Try another card," Jake suggested.

Rachel fanned out the deck and pulled out the Ace of Cups. When she smiled, Jake stroked his hand over her shoulder. "The start of a great love," he murmured.

"You're learning the cards."

"I like knowing what you know."

"A great love—ours or theirs."

"Let's see one more card," Jake said.

Rachel pulled out the Five of Swords and caught her breath.

"What?"

"Well, it usually means you are defeated, cheated out of victory by a cunning and underhanded opponent."

"You think it refers to that other couple?"

"Or to the person who is going against them and us. But sometimes with the Five of Swords, you are that victor. You're the one who wins over your opponents by using your mind."

"That sounds like us."

"And them."

"And you still don't have enough information to trust them?"

She shook her head. "It's not just us who would be at risk. It's also Gabriella and Luke," she said, referring to Gabriella Bordeaux and Luke Buckley, another couple who'd been born as a result of treatments at the Solomon Clinic. Rachel and Jake had come to their rescue, and they had formed a little community, using the plantation property Gabriella had inherited from her mother. Rachel and Jake lived there part of each week and commuted to New Orleans so that they could each maintain their business interests in the city, Rachel with her shop and Jake with his antiques and restaurant businesses.

"Can you at least try to figure out where they are?"

Rachel closed her eyes and leaned back in her chair, sending her mind outward.

"If Mrs. Dubour won't talk to us, we're no worse off than we were before," Craig said.

They drove away from town, turning off onto a secondary road that led to a small community at the edge of the bayou, checking the house numbers on the mailboxes as they drove.

When they came to number 529, they turned into a rutted gravel drive that was about fifty yards long. At the end was a white clapboard house with blue shutters surrounded by a trimmed lawn and neatly tended flower gardens edged with white painted rocks.

A car was parked in front, and they pulled up behind it and walked to the front porch that spanned the front of the house.

It took several moments for them to hear movement inside after they knocked. Finally an old woman opened the door. She looked to be in her late seventies, with wispy gray hair and a lined face. She was wearing slippers and a faded housedress.

"I'm not buying anything," she said as she stared through the screen door. "And I'm not interested in any religious lectures."

Stephanie shook her head. "We're not selling or preaching. Are you Mrs. Dubour?"

"Yes."

"We'd like to talk to you about your son, David."

She stiffened. "What about him?"

"We're staying at Mrs. Marcos's bed-and-breakfast, and we were talking to her this morning. She told us that you were treated at the Solomon Clinic before David was born."

"What about it?"

"Our mothers were both treated at the same clinic, and we wanted to find out what you knew."

Her expression had become less hostile as she'd listened to Stephanie speak. "I guess you'd better come in," she said.

Craig let out the breath he'd been holding as the older woman stepped aside. They followed her into a small, neat sitting room furnished in old maple pieces and a bulky sofa and overstuffed chairs.

"Sit down," she said, gesturing toward the sofa.

They sat, and she took one of the chairs opposite, where she watched them with speculative interest.

"You say your mothers went to the same clinic that I did?"

"Yes."

"How do you know?"

"It goes back to my twin brother being killed by mobsters in a restaurant when I was eight."

The old woman sucked in a sharp breath. "I'm so sorry."

"After Sam died, I remember hearing my mother trying to contact someone at the Solomon Clinic, but it was already closed by then."

"She wanted to have another child?"

"That's my guess."

"Weren't there other clinics she could have gone to?"

"Maybe she only had faith in Dr. Solomon."

"Yes, he had a way of projecting strength and reassurance."

Stephanie got back to the original question. "We looked through some of my mother's papers and found literature and application forms from the clinic."

"And how did the two of you get together?" Mrs. Dubour asked.

"I got some information on who might have caused my brother's death. I came down to New Orleans to investigate and found Stephanie," Craig explained, giving an abbreviated version of how they'd happened to hook up.

The old woman looked from one of them to the other. "Did you think it was odd that the two of you ended up meeting each other?"

"I wasn't thinking about it," Craig said.

Mrs. Dubour shook her head. "Maybe you should have," she said in a hard voice.

Craig kept his gaze fixed on her. She looked like a typical aging housewife, but she obviously had spent a lot of time thinking about what happened to her son. And she'd come to some interesting conclusions.

"Something similar happened with my David."

They both stared at her. "What do you mean?"

"David was living at home and working at the hardware store in Houma when he got an email from a woman who said she'd gotten his name from a lawyer who was investigating inequalities in fees charged at the Solomon Clinic. She said her mother had paid thousands to be treated there, and his mother had gotten her treatment for free. The woman was all hot under the collar, and she came charging down here to see David. She was a weird, kind of flighty girl. I took a dislike to her right away, but as soon as she and David locked eyes on each other, something changed with him. With both of them, I guess. I mean, you could see sparks flying between him and that girl."

"What was her name?" Craig asked.

"Penny Whitman."

"What happened?"

"I saw them outside under the willow tree, holding hands and looking like they'd been hit by a meteor or something, like they were having some kind of secret communication nobody else could tune in on."

Craig nodded, understanding perfectly.

"David was so happy. I'd never seen him like that before. They took off, and I never saw David alive again. He and the girl were found in a motel room in bed together— both of them dead."

Stephanie sucked in a sharp breath. "What happened to them?"

"The coroner said it was like both of them had had a cerebral hemorrhage."

"My God," Stephanie whispered.

"I'm sorry for your loss," Craig said.

Mrs. Dubour nodded. "Losing him would have been more of a shock if I hadn't felt that I'd lost him years ago. Or that he never really belonged to us."

"What do you mean?" Stephanie asked.

"I was so excited to have a child," she said, her voice low and wistful. "But he never was, you know, normal. He always kept to himself. He wasn't affectionate with me or my husband. He never did date much when he was a teenager." She gave both of them a sharp look. "Am I telling you things you understand about yourselves?"

"Yes," Stephanie whispered.

Craig also nodded in agreement.

She kept looking at them. "But you met each other, and something changed for you?"

"Yes."

"You went off together, like my David and that girl, only it turned out different for you."

"Yes," Craig said.

"You're alive, and he's dead."

"I'm sorry he died."

"Because he hooked up with that woman. Why did it kill them?"

Craig wasn't going to tell her that it had to do with forming a telepathic bond that might overwhelm the two people involved.

"I don't know," he said.

Mrs. Dubour kept her gaze on them. "I guess you two should be careful."

"Yes," Stephanie whispered, although Craig knew from her mind that she was sure they had made it past the dangerous phase of bonding.

"Did you ever find out anything about the lawyer who sent the woman down here?"

"I didn't pursue it."

"Do you happen to know his name," he pressed.

She hesitated, probably coping with all the sad memories he and Stephanie had dredged up. It would be kindest to let her be, but because they had come here for information, Craig gave her a push. *If you know who the lawyer was, you should tell us. We'd really appreciate the information.*

She was silent for several more moments, then said, "She came down here with the email."

"You mean from the lawyer?"

"Yes." Mrs. Dubour got to her feet and left the room. While she was gone, they both waited tensely, wondering if she'd really be able to put her hands on the evidence. Finally she returned holding a piece of paper. "Here it is."

When she handed over the paper, Craig scanned it. It was from a Lewis Martinson in Washington, D.C.

"Thank you so much," Stephanie said. "We really appreciate this."

They talked to Mrs. Dubour for a few more minutes. When the woman stood up, her shoulders slumped.

"I'm sorry to have brought all this up for you," Stephanie murmured.

"I hope it does some good."

When they were back in the car, Stephanie turned to him, and he felt the relief in her mind.

"We could have ended up like David and that woman."

"Yeah."

"We both had a headache when we first made love. I guess that was a symptom of…"

"Getting ready to have a stroke," he finished for her.

"What was the difference for them?"

"We can't know for sure. Maybe the pain was too much for them to focus on the pleasure. Maybe they lost their nerve at the last minute, and when they didn't bond, they'd already set the process in motion."

When he saw a shiver go through her, he reached for her hand, holding tight.

"We got through it," she said. "Thank God we didn't understand the danger."

"I guess it's a crap shoot—how it turns out," he said.

"I prefer to think that we had something they didn't."

He laughed. "We were hornier."

She grinned, then sobered. "It looks like somebody wanted to get David and that woman together. Maybe to find out what would happen."

"I don't like being manipulated."

"Likewise. How did you happen to come down to New Orleans?"

"I never gave up the idea of finding out who was responsible for Sam's death, which was one of the reasons I maintained connections with police departments all over the U.S."

"Interesting that the body turned up after all these years."

"You think…"

He let his voice trail off, but he knew where her mind was going. Somebody had deliberately arranged for him to receive the information because they wanted him to come down to New Orleans and investigate the man responsible for Sam's death—which would mean that he would meet Stephanie Swift.

"Which meant they knew investigating John Reynard would lead you to me," she murmured. Then she added, "It's someone who knows there's something…strange about the children from the clinic." She looked at him. "How, exactly, did you find out about Arthur Polaski?"

"I got a call from a contact at the New Orleans P.D., Ike Broussard."

"You think he's working with Lewis Martinson?"

"I'll be surprised if it's that simple."

"Then what are we going to do?"

"We could talk to Broussard and look up Martinson. Unless you want to go poking around in Houma."

She thought about that. "I think that would be danger-ous, because Martinson already knows we're likely to come to Houma."

"Agreed."

"And I wouldn't have any more contact with Broussard."

"You could be right about that."

They stopped to pick up lunch at a fast-food restaurant, then returned to the bed-and-breakfast, where Craig booted up his computer and looked up Lewis Martinson. There were several people with that name, but none of them was a lawyer in Washington, D.C.

"Now what?" Stephanie asked.

"I'm thinking."

Chapter Fourteen

Ike Broussard swiped his shirtsleeve across his forehead and sat for a moment in his unmarked car, postponing the moment of reckoning. A lawyer in Washington, D.C., had paid him to make sure a guy named Craig Branson got some information about a cold case. Now he was realizing that he could have put his balls in a wringer.

He'd thought John Reynard would never know who had given Branson the information. But somehow it had gotten back to him, and now Ike was in deep kimchi.

Finally he opened the car door and hoisted his two-hundred-fifty-pound bulk to the cracked sidewalk.

He didn't count it as a good sign that Reynard had asked to meet him at one of his warehouses.

He buttoned his sports jacket over his bulging middle, then decided it looked better unbuttoned.

Glancing up at the redbrick building, he saw that a couple of video cameras were tracking his approach to the warehouse door. So if he didn't come out of here alive, would Reynard destroy the tapes?

Trying to look confident, he walked through the door, which led directly onto a dimly lit space half the size of a football field stacked with boxes. But there were no men working the forklifts that sat along the left wall. He looked upward, locating the metal balcony on the other side of the room. Up there was an office where he'd been told to meet Reynard.

His footsteps echoed on the cement floor as he crossed the room, then clanged on the metal stairs. At the top, he looked toward the lit office.

Two bodyguards were in the waiting area. They gave him a knowing look as he knocked on the door to the inner office.

"Come in," Reynard called out.

His heart was pounding as he went in.

"Close the door."

He did as the import-export man asked.

"Thank you for coming," Reynard said.

Ike nodded.

"I assume you thought I wouldn't find out who told Branson about Polaski."

When Ike started to speak, he waved him to silence. "You made a mistake. Every man is entitled to one mistake."

The observation didn't stop the pounding of his heart.

"But you have a chance to redeem yourself," Reynard said.

Ike waited to find out what he had to do.

"I want the location of Branson's cell phone."

Ike didn't bother saying that giving out information was against the law. He only said, "Yes, sir."

"I want it by the end of the day," Reynard clarified. "And when you've got it, you're going to do something else for me."

AT THE COTTAGE, Craig pushed back his chair and stood up.

"What now?" Stephanie asked.

When he sent her a very explicit picture, she flushed. "Is that all you think about?"

"I'm a guy. When I'm locked in a room with a beautiful woman, I can't help thinking about making love to her."

"You're not locked in."

"Not technically, but I think we need to stay out of sight. Which means staying in here. Do you have a better suggestion for how to use the time?"

"Do you think Dr. Solomon was trying to create telepaths?" she asked.

"I don't know."

"It's kind of a stretch."

He nodded.

'So what if he was trying to do something else, and this is what happened?'"

"Work before pleasure. Let's do more research on the Solomon Clinic and see if we can figure it out."

"This is the address," Tommy Ladreau said.

"Like the boss said, it's a bed-and-breakfast." He looked behind him at another car that had pulled up. It was a detective from the New Orleans P.D., a guy named Ike Broussard, and Tommy didn't like having him on the scene. But it had been the boss's orders.

"We don't know if they're in the main house or one of the cottages," his partner, Marv Strickland, said.

"Go see if you can spot his car."

Marv climbed out and made his way through the bushes to the main house, checking the cars in the parking spots. When Branson's car wasn't one of them, he started down the lane that wound through the property.

When he located Branson's rental, he stopped, then moved into the shrubbery again.

His orders were to bring Stephanie Swift back, and if he had to kill Craig Branson to do it, so be it. But Marv was hoping to avoid an outright murder in broad daylight.

He went back to the car and climbed into the passenger seat.

"You saw him?"

"I saw his car."

"Tell Broussard to do his thing."

Marv climbed out again and walked back to the car behind theirs.

"Go for it," he said.

CRAIG AND STEPHANIE came up with several more articles about the clinic, but nothing that would tell them what Dr. Solomon had been doing.

"I'm wondering if he was operating with government funding," Craig said.

"What about it?"

"That might be a way to get a line on whoever's after us."

"We also have the names of several women who worked there," Stephanie said. "Nurses."

"Yeah." Craig thought about that. "What if I talk to some of them? There's one who's living in a nursing home in Houma, for example."

"What do you mean—you? If you're going, so am I."

"You're the one who pointed out that it was dangerous to go into Houma."

"Yes, but…"

"You stay here, and I'll be back in a couple of hours."

"Don't go unless you know she's really there."

"Okay." He looked up the number and dialed the nursing home, asking if he could speak to Mrs. Bolton.

"She's not feeling well this evening," the woman who answered the phone said.

He felt Stephanie's sigh of relief.

"So you don't have to go see her."

Almost as soon as Craig clicked off, his cell phone rang and they both went rigid.

"Who could that be?"

He looked at the unfamiliar number.

"Don't answer."

"I'd better do it."

When he clicked the phone, the man on the other end of the line turned out to be Ike Broussard, the police detective who was responsible for his trip to New Orleans.

"Branson?" he said.

"Yes."

"I've got some information for you."

"What?"

"Not over the phone. I want you to meet me."

"Where?"

"At the Bayou Restaurant in Houma."

"You know about the Houma connection?"

"Uh-huh."

"What do you have for me?"

"I'll tell you when I see you."

"Something to do with the Solomon Clinic?"

The detective hesitated for a moment, then said, "Yeah."

"Okay."

He clicked off and looked at Stephanie.

I'll be back as soon as I can.

I was hoping you wouldn't leave.

I know.

He reached for her, and she came into his arms, clinging tightly. "I just found you. I don't know what I'd do if I lost you."

"You won't lose me."

They held each other for long moments, and he had to force himself to ease away.

"I'll be back as soon as I can."

He stepped outside the door of the cottage and stood for a moment, feeling the barrier between them. He couldn't see Stephanie now, but he could still feel her mind, and that was comforting. Even when he walked to the car and climbed in, he was still in contact with her.

Craig, he heard her whisper his name.

I don't like leaving you.

Then don't.

He didn't answer because there was nothing he could say. Still, he had to fight the need to turn around and go back as the contact with her faded and then vanished altogether.

He flashed back to the horrible moment when Sam had died and the contact between them had snapped.

This was the same, only Stephanie wasn't dead; she was just out of range. He would finish his mission and come back to the cottage, and she would be there waiting for him.

He turned on the engine and drove away, heading for the restaurant where Broussard had said he was waiting.

STEPHANIE WALKED BACK to the bedroom, where she and Craig had made love. While they'd been out, Mrs. Marcos had remade the bed.

Stephanie sat down, smoothing her hand across the spread, thinking that if she folded back the spread and climbed under the covers she'd feel closer to Craig. Maybe she could just sleep until he came back.

A knock at the door interrupted her thoughts.

"I'll be right there," she called out as she walked into the living room. Thinking it was someone from the B and B staff, she opened the door.

The two men she'd seen in the car across the street from her house barreled in, a mixture of triumph and relief on their faces.

As CRAIG DROVE into Houma, he kept alert for the men who had kidnapped him and Stephanie. He'd struggled to keep his thoughts to himself as he'd discussed this trip with Stephanie, but now that he was alone, he was aware that he was at risk. And as he thought about it, he couldn't be sure if Lieutenant Broussard was on the up-and-up. He drove slowly past the Bayou Restaurant, looking in the window, trying to spot Broussard. Although he'd never met the man, he was pretty sure he could identify a police detective.

But as he glanced in his rearview mirror, he saw a van in back of him, a van a lot like the one the two thugs had used when they'd kidnapped him and Stephanie.

He cursed aloud, speeding up, wishing he knew the city better. He'd insisted that Stephanie stay at the B and B, and now he realized he'd given up the one advantage he'd had. Together he and Stephanie had psychic powers they could draw on. Alone, he was the way he'd been for all the years since Sam had died.

He drove across a bridge that spanned a bayou, then across another, surprised at how much water flowed through the city. The van stayed behind him as he turned down a side street, then came to a screeching halt when the blacktop ended at the bank of a river.

There was nowhere to back up, no escape in his vehicle. Throwing open the door, he sprang out and started running along the edge of the bayou.

He heard running feet behind him and then the sound of a bullet whizzing past his head.

He ran down a short pier, then dived in, swimming deep underwater as more shots were fired. His only option was to keep going, trying to put as much distance between himself and the men with the guns while he veered downstream to make it harder for them to figure out where he would surface.

Finally, when his lungs were bursting, he swam to the surface and dragged in air.

He heard a shout, then bullets hit the water around him, but he was already diving.

He let the current carry him farther downstream. When he came up again, low-hanging branches shielded him from view.

Looking back, he saw the two men running along the bank, but it appeared that neither one of them was going to plunge into the bayou.

When he heard a splash, he looked to his right and saw an alligator slipping into the water.

Teeth gritted, he used a cypress root to pull himself out of the water, putting a tree trunk between himself and the men with the guns.

His clothing was dripping. His shoes were covered with mud, and he was out in the open. If he turned around, he would likely run into the men.

His only option was to keep walking, his shoes sucking in the mud as he put space between himself and the two men. He had left civilization behind. There was only dense vegetation on both sides of the water, cypress and tupelo and saw palmetto, until he came to a shack near the water. In front of it was a pier, and tied to the pier was a pirogue, one of the small boats that the local residents used.

He looked behind him and across the water. The men had lost him in the swamp, and he thought it would be safe to cross the water again. The shack in front of him looked deserted.

Turning toward the pier, he walked onto the weathered boards, heading for the boat.

Before he had gotten more than a few feet, a voice rang out behind him.

"You—hold up, or you're a dead man."

STEPHANIE FACED the two men, determined not to give them anything Reynard could use against her. "Thank God you're here."

"Oh, yeah? Looks like you were pretty cozy here with Branson."

"I thought his name was Craig Brady."

"Craig Branson," one of the men corrected.

"He was using a false name?" she answered, as if she was shocked.

"What were you doing here with him?" the shorter man asked.

"He was holding me captive."

"What did he want with you?"

"I'll talk to Mr. Reynard about that," she said, hoping she could come up with a story he would believe.

The guy snorted, and Stephanie fought to project the impression that she was telling the truth.

"Come on, we're getting out of here."

"Going where?"

"Mr. Reynard is waiting for you."

"Let me get my stuff."

He hesitated for a moment, and she struggled to project the idea that he had to give her a few more minutes here—time to leave a clue for Craig.

CRAIG TURNED to see a grizzled old man with a week's growth of beard, wearing a camouflage shirt, torn blue jeans and combat boots. He was holding a shotgun pointed at Craig's chest.

"Don't shoot. I need help," Craig said, raising his hands above his head.

The guy's face turned a shade less hostile as he took in Craig's appearance. "What happened to you?"

"Two guys with guns were chasing me."

"Yeah, why?"

Craig took a chance and asked, "Have you heard of the Solomon Clinic?"

"You one of the bastards who was runnin' that place?"

Craig shook his head. "I'm one of the children who was born as a result of Dr. Solomon's treatments. Somebody knows about us and is going after us."

The guy lowered the rifle. "Yeah. My nephew was one of them kids. He's dead."

Craig sucked in a sharp breath.

"He was one of the ones who got together with another kid from the clinic—and croaked in bed with her."

"I think my…girlfriend and I lucked out on that part. But somebody's been chasing us since we met."

"Where is she?"

"I left her at a B and B outside of town and came here to talk to a police detective who said he had some information for me."

"Don't never trust the cops."

Craig was already having bad feelings about Broussard. "You may be right."

His benefactor said, "You need dry clothes and a ride."

"I'd surely appreciate it," Craig allowed.

"I think I got something from my son that you can wear." He turned and walked toward the shack.

Craig followed, sloshing as he went, then hesitated at the doorway.

"I'll get your place wet."

"The water will go through the cracks in the floor. Come on in."

Craig followed the man inside. The interior looked a lot more comfortable than the ramshackle facade suggested. A lantern sat on a wooden table, illuminating a narrow bed, several chairs and a small kitchen area, all neatly arranged.

The old man opened a chest of drawers and pulled out a shirt like the one he was wearing and another pair of jeans.

Craig shucked off his wet clothing and put on the dry replacements. The pant legs were an inch too short, but they were better than what he'd been wearing. His shoes were still a muddy mess, but there was nothing he could do about that at the moment. His cell phone was ruined, and his wallet was soggy, but the money and credit cards inside would dry out.

"You got a way to get back to your place?" his benefactor asked.

"I left my car on the other side of the river," Craig answered.

"I can take you across."

They walked down the dock where Craig climbed into the boat and the old man cast off, using a paddle to propel them.

Craig looked back, seeing the dense swampy area where the shack was almost hidden from view.

"Thank you," he said when they got to the other side. As he reached for his wallet, the old Cajun shook his head.

"No need."

Craig climbed out and started along the shore, watching for the men who had chased him. It seemed they had given up the chase for the moment, but what about Stephanie? He made it to his vehicle and climbed in, torn between caution and speeding as he headed back to the B and B.

He wanted to rush to the cottage, but instinct had him stopping down the block and proceeding on foot, casting his thoughts before him, trying to contact Stephanie. He knew she had to be worried—and probably angry that he'd left her alone.

There was no mental sign from her as he approached the cottage, and he felt his chest tighten.

Then he saw something that stopped him in his tracks. It was Ike Broussard climbing out of a car and heading for the cottage.

As far as Craig knew, the bastard hadn't kept the appointment at the restaurant. What was he doing here now?

Craig sped up, calling out a mental warning to Stephanie as he watched the man push open the front door.

He'd barely disappeared inside when a massive explosion shook the little building, throwing Craig to the ground.

Chapter Fifteen

Craig covered his head with his arms as debris rained down around him. As soon as he could, he scrambled to his feet and ran toward the building.

"Stephanie. Oh, Lord, Stephanie," he called out as he surveyed the damage. The building simply wasn't there, and the man who had stepped inside had vanished.

Craig's whole body was shaking. He'd left Stephanie here when she'd begged him to take her with him. He'd thought he was doing the right thing, and now she was gone—the way Sam was gone. That had been the worst thing that had ever happened to him. This was a thousand times worse.

He heard a siren in the distance. The fire department and probably the cops. Instinct told him to get the hell out of there before the authorities arrived.

Quickly he backed away and ran down the block to the spot where he'd left his car.

"SHE'S IN THE CAR. We're on our way," the man in the back-seat said into his cell phone. He listened for a minute, then said, "We expect to be there in forty-five minutes."

Stephanie knew that John Reynard had a number of residences. One was a plantation house about forty miles from New Orleans. Which was where they were going, Stephanie surmised.

After one of the men had hustled her out of the cottage, the other had gotten something out of the trunk and gone back to the cottage, but she'd had no idea what he was doing.

He'd given his partner the thumbs-up when he'd climbed back into the car. Then the three of them had sped away. Toward her doom? Or could she somehow save herself—and get back to Craig?

She modified that thought. She had to get back to Craig. She belonged with him, not with the man she'd promised to marry because of misplaced loyalty to her father.

She'd felt guilty about her relationship with him, and she'd told herself that was her fault. Now she knew it wasn't true. It had as much to do with him as with her, and it was too bad she hadn't seen that a long time ago.

But her father wasn't her immediate problem. *That* was John Reynard. Every time the car slowed to take a curb or stop at a traffic light, she thought about jumping out and making a run for it. But that would only confirm her guilt. And what was the chance that she could actually evade these men?

She would have to face John, but what could she say to him that he would want to hear—and that he'd believe?

It was hard to make her mind work coherently, and she was still trying to figure out what she was going to say when the car stopped at the gate across the access road. Once the house had sat in the middle of cotton fields. Now it was a fortified compound, guarded by men and a fence that circled the area around the house.

The barrier slid open, letting the car through, then slid closed behind her—like a prison gate clanging shut. The long drive was lined with live oak trees, making a majestic approach to the restored plantation house that had been newly painted white. It had a portico across the front that reminded Stephanie of Tara in *Gone with the Wind,* except that the entrance was on the second floor as in most Louisiana plantation houses.

When the car pulled up beside the wide front steps, Stephanie dragged in a breath and let it out, preparing for what was coming next.

Unable to move, she simply sat in the passenger seat.

"Get out," the man in back said, climbing out and opening her door.

There was no point in trying to stay in the car. It wouldn't do her any kind of good. She climbed out and stood on shaky legs, looking up at the steps.

When a figure appeared, she blinked. It was Claire Dupree, the woman who had been helping her in the dress shop for the past few months. Once the shop had been her life, but she hadn't thought about her business or her assistant in days. Now she tipped her head as she stared at Claire.

"What are you doing here?" she asked.

"John thought you'd appreciate having some female companionship."

"John asked you here?"

"Yes."

As Stephanie tried to work her way through the implications, a lightbulb suddenly went off in her head. Claire had come to the shop looking for a job not long after Stephanie had met John Reynard. She'd offered to work for almost no salary.

Now it was pretty clear why. Stephanie had been paying her a small salary, but she'd really been working for John Reynard. He'd sent her to Stephanie so that he could keep tabs on his fiancée.

"We've been waiting for you. Why don't you come in?"

Claire said, as if she was the owner of the house inviting in a guest.

With no other choice, Stephanie followed the other woman up the stairs and into the house, which had been furnished with many antebellum antiques as well as some comfortable modern pieces. The wide front hall boasted a sideboard imported from England with a gilt mirror hanging on the wall above. Like her father's house, but in much better condition. On the polished floorboards was a rich Oriental rug.

"Where's John?" she asked.

"He's in the lounge. There's some very interesting news on television."

The edge in Claire's voice made her wary, but she followed the other woman down the hall to the sitting room that John had set up like a room in a turn-of-the-century men's club, furnished with comfortable leather chairs and couches.

The walls were wood-paneled, and the only piece of furniture that looked out of character in the room was the flat-screen TV on the wall across from the sofa.

John, who had been sitting in one of the leather chairs, stood up.

He looked from her to the television, where an announcer was breathlessly reporting some catastrophe and it took Stephanie a few moments to orient herself. First she realized it was in Houma. Then she saw it was at a bed-and-breakfast. The reporter was pointing to what must have been a house or a cottage; nothing was left but a blackened hole in the ground.

"Police say there are no survivors from the explosion that destroyed one of the cottages at the Morning Glory B and B about an hour ago. At the time a Mr. and Mrs. Craig Branson were registered at the cottage."

Stephanie tried to take that in. In the background she could see the main building, and it looked as if the blackened ruin was the cottage where she and Craig had been staying.

"Sorry to report that your friend Craig Branson was blown up in an explosion while you were en route here," John said, the tone of his voice making it clear that he wasn't sorry at all.

Unable to catch her breath, Stephanie swayed on her feet. Claire caught her arm and eased her onto the couch, where she sat gasping for air.

John tipped his head to the side as he stared at her. "It isn't confirmed that your friend was in the cottage, but I presume that he rushed back home to you, opened the door and triggered an unfortunate incident."

"No," Stephanie whispered.

John glanced at Claire. "Go get Stephanie a glass of brandy. I believe she could use a drink."

Stephanie watched the other woman leave the room. Then she swung back to John when he said, "You're in a delicate position now."

She answered with a small nod, wondering exactly where this conversation was going. She was still struggling to come to grips with her new reality—back in the clutches of John Reynard. If it was her new reality. The explosion was real, but what if by some miracle Craig was all right?

She had to cling to that. It was her only option, because if she admitted that he was dead, what was the use of her going on? Or to put it another way, what did it matter what John Reynard did to her?

He was speaking, and she struggled to focus on his words. "So whatever you've been doing with him, it's over. And now we can take up where we left off."

"Yes," she managed to say.

"You refused to sleep with me until we were married," he said suddenly, his words and his tone lancing through the wall she had tried to build around her emotions. "A very old-fashioned attitude, I must say. Did you sleep with him?"

She should have been expecting the question. Well, perhaps not so bluntly. Now she froze, knowing that she was skating on very thin ice.

Raising her head, she looked John square in the eye, calling on all the salesmanship she'd learned at the dress shop. "No," she said aloud, and as she spoke, she did something else, as well—gathered her mental power and put it into her silent order to him. *You believe me. You believe I didn't sleep with Craig Branson. You believe it because you want to believe it. That's the answer you want to hear, and you believe me.*

Would it work? She certainly hadn't been able to do anything like that before she'd met Craig. The power had developed as a result of her connection to him.

A stray thought danced in her mind, a thought that gave her hope. Or was it false hope?

She brushed aside that last part. If she'd developed this power with Craig, could she still use it if he was dead?

She clung to that as she kept shooting her silent message to John, and maybe her faith that Craig was still alive made the suggestion stronger.

HAROLD GODDARD HELD UP the duct tape he'd asked his man to leave for him at the shopping center. It was the tape that had been used to restrain Swift and Branson. It was stretched slightly out of shape, as if it had somehow been melted. How had that happened? Had Branson or Swift done something to it? And if so, what and how? The speculation was cut off when his cell phone rang. He put down the tape and clicked the on button.

"You have them?"

"No," Wayne answered.

"You followed him, but you weren't able to get your hands on him?" Harold clarified.

"We had him cornered, but he dived into the bayou."

"And then what?"

The man on the other end of the line hesitated, and Harold could picture the scene.

"Did you shoot him?" he asked.

"We tried to wound him, but he got away."

"And he didn't go back to the bed-and-breakfast?"

Again the man seemed reluctant to answer. Finally he said, "When we didn't find him, we went back to the place where they were staying."

"And?"

"There was an explosion," Wayne said.

Harold shouted a curse into the phone. He walked across the room and snapped on a news channel. A breathless reporter was giving the details of a mysterious explosion in Houma.

"I'll get back to you later." Harold advised.

"You want us to stay in Houma?"

"Yes." He clicked off and focused on the report. It seemed that the man and woman who had rented the cottage were Craig Branson and his wife. Unless they'd gotten married in the past couple of days, that was a polite fiction.

But were they really dead?

He'd keep checking to see if they surfaced somewhere. Meanwhile, he'd look around for another couple he could send into each other's arms.

FOR THE SECOND TIME in his life, Craig Branson was completely devastated. Sam's death had almost killed him. He'd survived. But now he was facing unimaginable heartbreak.

He had no idea where he was going as he put distance between himself and the terrible explosion. He simply drove aimlessly, wanting to get away from the place where Stephanie had died.

Moisture clouded his vision, and he finally pulled over to the side of the road, thinking that he was a menace to other drivers if he couldn't see straight.

He sat for long moments, gripping the wheel and trying to get his emotions under control. But grief rolled over him, drowned him, making him wonder if there was any use going on without Stephanie. What if he just drove his car into a bayou? There would be no one to miss him. No one to mourn him.

He'd lived his life a certain way because he'd thought he'd never find a woman he could love. Never marry. He'd found Stephanie, and it had been wonderful, except for the serious complications. Not just because she was supposed to marry the man responsible for his brother's death, but because someone had tried to kidnap them. He'd tried to find out who it was and hadn't succeeded. It flickered through his mind that figuring out who they were would give him a goal.

If he could pull himself together again. For the moment, he was too paralyzed with grief.

He started to swing back onto the highway, then stopped short as a car horn blared, and he realized he'd almost plowed into another vehicle.

Sorry, he mouthed when the other driver gave him the finger. After that he drove slowly to the next town and found a downscale motel where he could hole up.

He debated using his credit card, then decided that if he was supposed to be dead, maybe staying dead was the best way to go, for now. He paid in cash, then pulled back the covers on the lumpy bed and threw himself down, wondering how long he was going to be there and what he was going to do next.

He let the notion of getting a gun and shooting himself swirl around in his head. That was what you did with an animal in pain, wasn't it? It had a lot of appeal, but at the same time he hated the idea of giving up everything he had ever worked for.

Yeah, but what was it worth now? Without Stephanie.

JAKE HARPER CRADLED his wife in his arms. An hour earlier, Rachel had been struck by a thunderbolt. Not literally, but the effect was the same. She'd been standing in the kitchen loading the dishwasher when something had made her whole body jerk. Thank God he'd been there to catch her and take the plate out of her hand when she'd fallen.

He'd picked her up in his arms and asked her what was wrong, but she hadn't been able to answer him, either aloud or in her mind. So he'd struggled to suppress his own fear as he cradled her in his lap and rocked her, waiting until the storm passed and she was able to function again.

Finally she raised her head and looked around as though she didn't recognize her surroundings—although they were in one of the apartments Jake owned in New Orleans. Long ago he'd gotten into the habit of moving around the city. He had several comfortably furnished places, and he and Rachel split their time among them and the plantation in Lafayette where Gabriella Bordeaux and Luke Buckley lived. With funding from Jake, Gabriella had turned her family's plantation house into a showcase restaurant called Chez Gabriella. She and Luke lived upstairs in the plantation house, and Rachel and Jake had one of the cottages on the property, where they stayed part of the week. All four of them were children from the Solomon Clinic. And all four of them often joined forces to practice their psychic powers together.

Jack stroked Rachel's hair. "What happened?" he asked.

"There was an explosion near Houma. Turn on the television set."

Jake picked up the remote from the end table and clicked on a news channel. Instantly, they were in the middle of a breathless report from the affiliate in Houma.

"It is believed that Mr. and Mrs. Craig Branson were killed in the explosion that destroyed a cottage at the Morning Glory B and B," the reporter was saying. "Authorities are still not sure what caused the explosion."

"A bomb," Rachel whispered.

Jake shuddered. "And the couple are dead?"

Rachel closed her eyes and pressed her fingers against her forehead. "No."

He stared at her. "What happened?"

She dragged in a breath and let it out. "They escaped. Craig was out trying to get some information about the Solomon Clinic. Stephanie…"

"Their names are Craig and Stephanie?"

"Craig Branson and Stephanie Swift."

Jake's eyes narrowed. "Doesn't she have a dress shop on Royal Street?"

"Yes."

"And…isn't she supposed to marry a nasty piece of work named John Reynard?"

Rachel nodded. "Yes. Only that was her father's idea. Then she met Craig, and she knew she couldn't marry Reynard." Rachel gripped her husband's hand. "Reynard found out where she and Craig were staying. He found a way to get Craig out of the house. He kidnapped Stephanie and had his men set the cottage to explode when Craig came home. Only someone else set off the bomb."

"And you know all this—how?" Jake asked in a rough voice.

"It…came to me." She looked at her husband. "Stephanie and Craig each think the other is dead. Both of them are devastated. Think about how you'd feel if you thought I was…gone."

"Don't say that."

"I'm trying to make you understand why this is so urgent."

Jake's chest tightened as he imagined his own grief if he somehow lost Rachel.

He knew she followed his thoughts and emotions, knew from the way she wrapped her arms around him and from her own churning mind that she was imagining the same terrible situation—in reverse.

We can't leave them like that, she silently whispered.

We agreed that contacting them could be dangerous, Jake argued.

Are you saying you can leave them in so much pain?

Jake let the question sink in. *No. What do you want to do?*

They're far apart now. I think I can boost the signal between them. Let them talk to each other.

She turned to her husband. *But I can't do it alone. Will you help me?*

He hesitated, caught by the urgency of her request and the need to keep both of them safe. Not just themselves, but Gabriella and Luke, too.

They'd made a commitment to the other couple; now Rachel was saying they should act on their own.

Can't we wait?

They might go mad or kill themselves if we just wait.

Chapter Sixteen

Stephanie rarely drank anything stronger than wine. Now she sipped the brandy John had given her, welcoming the fiery sensations as it slid down her throat. Wanting to be alone with her private agony, she kept her gaze focused on the television, hoping against hope for some scrap of news that would tell her Craig had survived the blast.

"We should move up the wedding," John was saying. "I want the chance to be close to you, to make up for what you've just been through."

Her gaze swung to him, and she knew he was watching for her reaction to that bit of news.

"Yes," she said.

"We can have the ceremony here at the plantation. We'll just invite a few friends—and your father, of course. I'm thinking a morning ceremony, then lunch around the pool."

She nodded numbly. Was there any escape from this lovely plantation that was really a fortress? And where would she go if she could get away? It would have to be somewhere John could never find her. Out of the country for sure, but why bother if Craig was dead?

"Claire has been very helpful. She's been making a guest list, which she'll share with you. And she tells me that your wedding dress arrived at your shop."

"Yes."

"I'll arrange to have it delivered here."

"And we can contact a catering company," Claire added brightly. "And a florist. That's all you need."

"And a license and man of God," John added. "But all that's easy to arrange." He made a dismissive wave of his hand.

She tried to take all that in. Everything was moving too fast, and she wanted to scream at John to slow down, but she had to act as if she loved the idea of marrying him right away—because anything less was dangerous.

And then what? She imagined kissing him. Imagined his hands on her body, and she had to keep herself from screaming.

As she fought to look normal, something happened that made her head spin, and she gasped.

John tensed. "Stephanie, what?"

She tried to speak, but she couldn't get the words out. John's face swam before her, and she saw the panic in his eyes.

"I'm sick. Migraine headache. Need to lie down," she whispered.

"I didn't know you had migraines."

Neither did I, she thought, but she only said, "Yes."

Because she needed to be alone. Now.

JOHN HELPED STEPHANIE to the bedroom, taking in her pale face as she kicked off her shoes. She looked sick. No doubt about it, but he was having trouble believing anything she said now.

She hadn't slept with Brandon? He wanted it to be true, but he couldn't be sure.

She was such a beautiful, desirable woman—from an old family that had seen better days. Probably her social standing had been one of the reasons he'd been willing to wait until marriage to make love to her. That and the convenience of having Claire as a willing bed partner. It had amused him to sleep with the woman who was spying on his fiancée. He'd even entertained some fantasies of taking the two of them to bed. He knew Claire would be totally okay with that. Maybe it would take some persuading to get Stephanie to agree.

She was a lady, and he'd thought she was adhering to what she considered proper.

His mind circled back to the moment when he'd decided to marry Stephanie Swift. It had been at one of the damn charity events that he was expected to attend. This time at the St. Charles Country Club. One of the other men there, Larry Dalton, had called him aside to ask about their business transaction. Larry had gone in with John on an import deal, two million dollars worth of heroin packed in toys coming in from Taiwan. Only someone must have tipped off the Feds because they'd sent in an inspector to check the shipment. And it had been the guy's bad luck.

John's men had caught him on the boat while it was at sea, and the federal agent had ended up overboard in the Pacific Ocean.

John had gotten a report about it before he'd left for the reception, and when Larry had approached him at the event, he'd been in a bad mood. He'd told him about it, watching the man's face as he realized he was a party to murder.

John had enjoyed spoiling the man's evening. And then he'd turned around and seen Stephanie Swift in back of him. Had she heard? He wasn't sure, and she certainly hadn't said anything, but he wasn't going to take a chance on her telling anyone about it. Which was why he'd started keeping her close.

He'd decided that if she married him, she couldn't testify against him, and he'd been glad when she'd agreed to the marriage, because he'd rather screw her than kill her. But maybe he was going to end up doing both.

Of course, now he had other things to think about. Like why had Branson been dragging her around? Had he talked about the long-ago death of his brother—and of Arthur Polaski? If she knew about any of that, she was more dangerous to him. But he'd find out after the wedding. After he took what she owed him.

CRAIG HAD DOZED OFF. He jerked awake when he heard a voice in his head. A woman's voice.

Craig Branson.

Hope flared inside him.

Stephanie? Oh, Lord, is that you, Stephanie?

No. I'm a friend.

He tried to cope with the instant wave of despair and with the confusion swirling in his mind. Had grief driven him mad, and he had invented an invisible friend to compensate for the loss of the woman he loved?

The voice pulled him back to her. *You aren't crazy. This is important.*

I doubt it.

Stephanie isn't dead.

His whole body went rigid as the words blasted into him, yet he couldn't allow himself to believe. Sitting up, he looked around the motel room, confirming he was alone.

Who are you? he repeated.

Rachel.

She was speaking to him—the way Sam had spoken to him. And Stephanie.

Do I know you? he asked in an inner voice that he couldn't quite hold steady.

No.

Is this a cruel joke?

No. I understand what you are suffering.

He scoffed at that statement. *How could you? How could anyone?*

Because I am one of the children from the Solomon Clinic, and I bonded with another one of us.

He made a low sound. Of course, he should have realized why she could reach his mind.

You must rescue Stephanie.

He scrambled off the bed, ready to charge out the door, if he only knew where he was going—and what had happened.

How did she escape?

Two of John Reynard's men captured her after you left. Then they set the explosive charge to kill you. Only someone else was caught in the blast.

Ike Broussard. I saw him. I didn't understand why he was there. He said he was going to meet me at a restaurant.

I think Reynard ordered him to meet you.

How do you know?

My husband knows which cops are corrupt in New Orleans. Ike Broussard was one of them.

Then why did he come to the cottage?

I can only guess at that. What if he hated being under Reynard's thumb and thought that the two of you could work together to take him down?

Craig considered that. It might fit the facts, and he was sorry the man was dead, but his main focus was Stephanie.

The woman named Rachel must have read his thoughts. *I can boost the signal between you.*

And then, all at once he caught Stephanie's silent voice. *Craig?*

Yes.

Oh, my God, you're alive! Reynard said you were dead. I'm fine.

Thank God, but how are we talking?

Someone's helping us. Another one of the children from the clinic.

Yes, I...heard her in my mind. I didn't know what was happening.

Where are you? Craig asked.

At the plantation Reynard owns, near Morgan City.

I'm on my way now.

Be careful. It's heavily guarded. With armed men.

We'll figure something out, he said, wondering what it was going to be.

*I can't hold the connection...*the woman who had made the long-distance contact between them said, and suddenly there was silence inside Craig's head—leaving him dazed and confused.

JAKE HARPER SWORE aloud as he picked up his wife from the couch. Lowering himself to a sitting position, he gathered her limp body in his arms.

"You hurt yourself," he whispered as he stroked his hands over her back and shoulders.

"I'm...okay," Rachel managed to say.

"You..."

She closed her eyes and clung to him. "They had information to give each other—and I was the only way they could do it."

"And now you're going to stay away from them," he said in a hard voice.

"They may need us."

"I'm not going to lose you because you feel some sort of obligation to two strangers."

She raised her head and looked at him. "Jake, they're two of Dr. Solomon's children."

"So were Tanya and Mickey," he bit out, referring to the telepaths who had tried to kill them.

"Craig and Stephanie are different. They're good people. They just want to be free to live their lives."

"So we can stay clear of them."

"Maybe that's not going to work."

"Maybe it has to," Jake said, punching out the words. He tipped Rachel's body so that she was looking up at him. "I was along for the ride on that mental conference call. Something you're not saying is that someone was after Craig. Not Reynard's men. There's something else going on."

He saw her swallow. "Yes."

"Maybe someone who knows about the clinic."

She gave a small nod.

"Wellington and Solomon are dead. So who is it?"

CRAIG BRACED HIS HAND against the wall, fighting to stay on his feet. His head was swimming as though he'd just suffered a blow to the jaw. But he didn't care.

He knew Stephanie was alive. And she knew he was okay, too. That was important, because Reynard had her, and if she thought Craig was dead, there was no telling what she'd do.

And he knew where she was. At least the general location. He started to charge out of the motel room, then checked himself. Men had chased him around Houma. If they didn't think he'd been blown up in that explosion, they would be searching for him again.

First he looked out the window to make sure nobody was lurking in the parking lot. Then he cautiously stepped outside.

He climbed into his car and used the GPS to set a course for Morgan City, driving below the speed limit so as not to call attention to himself. All he needed was to get stopped by a cop and have them find out he was still alive. If they did, they'd probably hold him for questioning in the death of Ike Broussard—when they found out he was the guy who'd gotten caught in the explosion.

Hopefully, that wasn't going to happen anytime soon because the big advantage Craig had now was that Reynard thought he was dead. If he could keep it that way, he'd have a better chance to get Stephanie out of there.

And then what? He'd worry about that after he sprang her.

When he reached the approximate vicinity, he stopped at one of the gas stations. After filling his tank, he went inside the station. As soon as he saw the racks of junk food, he realized he hadn't eaten anything since breakfast. He put a soft drink and some peanut-butter cheese crackers on the counter and paid for them, along with the gas, glad that he'd brought a fair amount of cash with him—and that he also had the use of the thugs' money. But eventually he was going to need more cash. Maybe he could rob the gas station, he thought with a snort before turning toward the cashier.

He ran his hand through his hair and looked around as if he thought the interior of the station would answer a vital question.

"I'm supposed to be delivering an important package to the Reynard estate," he said as he put his wallet back into his pocket, "but I'm not sure of the address. Can you tell me where it is?"

"It's about five miles south of town on the Old River Road," the man answered. "But you won't get in unless they're expecting you, because there's a guard at the gate."

"Thanks for the information," he said.

Before leaving town, he stopped at a dry-goods store and bought a tractor cap and a work shirt, which he put on in the men's room. He would have to stop to buy some more clothing, because he'd lost everything in the explosion. But he had brought his computer along in the car, which kept him from having to make a major purchase.

After doing what he could on short notice to disguise his appearance, he used the GPS to find Old River Road, then drove south. As the gas-station attendant had said, the Reynard estate was surrounded by a high chain-link fence, topped with razor wire, and a gate, with several men in attendance, controlling access to the property. As he drove past without stopping, he glimpsed a stately plantation house through the live oaks lining the drive.

How much surveillance equipment did Reynard have? he wondered as he put a mile between himself and the gate. Pulling off the road, into a small clearing, he tried to send his mind to Stephanie, but he was too far away and couldn't reach her.

He'd have to come back at night and hope that he could get close enough without alerting the guards.

A KNOCK AT THE DOOR made Stephanie go rigid. When the door opened, she expected to see John, but it was only Claire.

"How are you feeling?" her assistant asked.

"Better."

"Dinner is in an hour. I'm sure you want to look your best. Why don't you take a nice hot shower? And there are clothes in the closet."

"Thank you," she said as she climbed out of bed and headed for the bathroom, which turned out to be large and luxurious—a place she would have enjoyed if her stomach hadn't been tied in knots.

A shower and nice clothing. Was John thinking about

taking her to bed after dinner? If he was, she prayed she could derail that plan.

Once she'd showered, she dried her hair and tamed it into a style she knew John admired. Then she went to the closet to see what clothing was available.

There were a number of tasteful gowns and dresses, probably chosen by Claire, who was using the knowledge of style she'd learned at the shop.

Stephanie ground her teeth when she thought about her sweet little assistant. It went to show that you couldn't always tell a person's real motivations. She should have thought about that when she'd let John Reynard into her life. Well, it was too late to worry about what she should have done. She had to think carefully about what she was going to do now.

After looking through the dresses, she selected a pale green dinner gown, then did a careful job with her makeup, trying to present herself as the happy bride who had finally moved into the very well-appointed home of her fiancé.

But she hesitated at the door to her room, wishing she could stay locked away where John couldn't touch her.

"Stop it," she muttered to herself. "You have to face him, and you have to make him absolutely sure that you're relieved to be here."

After taking a deep breath and letting it out, she stepped into the hall and headed for the stairs.

John and Claire were waiting for her in the drawing room, sitting with their heads together, speaking in low voices. She stood for a moment in the doorway, observing the intimacy between them and confirming her earlier thought that they were probably sleeping together. That would have made her angry if she'd cared about her relationship with John Reynard. Under the circumstances, she couldn't help thinking that the other woman was doing her a big favor, letting John blow off sexual steam with her instead of his fiancée.

They stopped talking abruptly when they noticed her in the doorway, and she suspected they had been talking about her.

John looked her up and down, taking in the makeup and the dress she'd chosen.

"I must say, you look lovely, my dear," he said, getting up and coming over to plant a kiss on her cheek.

"Thank you."

"Can I offer you some wine? I remember you like Merlot."

"Yes," she answered. She wasn't going to drink much because she needed to keep her wits about her. But she'd gotten an idea when John had offered her a drink.

She looked toward the glass he'd left on the end table and saw amber liquid and ice cubes. Probably bourbon, which was his whiskey of choice.

Have some more bourbon, she silently told him. *Drink more bourbon. You want to drink a lot of it tonight—to celebrate your impending marriage.*

She waited with her heart pounding while he poured her a glass of the red wine, then hesitated for a moment at the bar.

Again she sent her message and felt a thrill of relief and satisfaction when he reached for the bottle of Jack Daniel's and poured himself a drink.

He brought her the wine, then did a double take when he realized he already had a glass of whiskey sitting on the side table. Quickly he took it away and put it in the sink.

"We should eat," he said. "Matilda has prepared a delicious dinner for your homecoming. All the Creole treats you love. We're starting with Oysters Bienville. Then we have jambalaya, and we're finishing with bananas Foster."

"That sounds wonderful," she said, when she wondered how she could swallow any of it.

Bring your drink, she told John, and he obliged her by picking up his glass and carrying it into the dining room.

They took their seats at the table, where the staff gave everybody speculative looks, and she wondered what had been going on between John and Claire. Had they flaunted their relationship, or had the servants simply picked up on the intimacy between them?

The maid brought the baked oysters, the shells resting on a bed of hot salt, then served each of them two.

As Stephanie started to scoop the contents out of the shell, using the small oyster fork, a jolt of mental energy made her hand shake and the shell clatter against the dish.

John gave her a sharp look. "What?"

"I…just touched the hot oyster shell by accident," she lied.

"Let me see."

"Really, it was just enough to startle me," she said as she held out her hand, fighting madly to stay calm.

Craig had just contacted her.

Sorry, he apologized.

Where are you? she asked as she bent to fork up the oyster in its creamy sauce, hoping her face wasn't flushed. Craig was close by. Close enough to contact her.

I'm at the edge of the plantation. Around back.

Be careful, she warned, marveling that he could speak to her from so far away. Maybe something that woman Rachel had done had boosted the signal between her and Craig.

I am being careful. I just wanted you to know I'm here.

She forced herself to eat the oyster, then smile at John. "This is so good."

"I'm glad you like it."

"I'd like some more wine," she said. *And you want more bourbon. Lots more bourbon.*

They finished the meal, and when they got up from the table, John approached her, putting his arm around her shoulder so that his fingers brushed the top of her breast.

She caught her breath, knowing that she was playing a dangerous game. The whiskey had made him amorous, but had he drunk enough to keep him from performing?

"Let's have a nightcap in the lounge," she murmured, reinforcing the invitation with a mental suggestion, which she expanded to include Claire. The longer she could keep the other woman with them, the longer she could keep John from pawing her, she hoped.

The three of them sat together in the lounge. To avoid conversation, she suggested, *Let's watch a movie.*

"I wanted…" John said, then trailed off as though he had forgotten that he was hot to take his fiancée to bed.

Stephanie silently pushed the movie idea as she brought everyone a drink.

John picked an action-adventure, which was better than something sexy. But he crowded against her on the sofa, his lips brushing her cheek and his hand touching her leg or the side of her breast.

She fought not to cringe as she kept making suggestions that he drink, and by the time the movie was over, he was unsteady on his feet. Yet he clamped his arm around her as they walked to the stairs.

Her heart was in her throat as she let him walk her up the steps. Inside she was screaming, *You're so sleepy. All you want to do is fall on your bed and sleep. You'll enjoy making love to Stephanie so much more when your head doesn't feel so fuzzy.*

She held her breath as they passed her room, then continued on to his.

He stood wavering in the doorway, and she helped him inside, easing him onto the bed. He closed his eyes as she pulled off his shoes. Then his eyes blinked open and focused on her.

"Did you hear me talking about that murder?" he asked.

"What?" she gasped. "What are you talking about?"

"At that reception at the…what was it…the St. Charles Club. You know, where we first met. I was talking to Larry Dalton about…you know."

Her heart was in her throat.

"I know what?"

"That drug-enforcement agent who went into the ocean when he was messing with my shipment from Taiwan."

"No," she breathed.

"Got to keep you close," he muttered, "in case you heard."

Her heart was already pounding so hard she could barely breathe. Then, as his hand reached for her, she felt her heart leap into her throat.

Chapter Seventeen

As John made a grab for Stephanie, she stepped out of the way.

Sleep. Just sleep. You need to sleep, and you'll feel so much better in the morning.

To her profound relief, he accepted the suggestion and sank into sleep, and she exited his room, then hurried to her own, her pulse pounding.

She'd thought he'd wanted to marry her because he wanted entrée into an old New Orleans family. Apparently it was more than that. It seemed he thought she'd overheard a conversation about a murder he'd ordered.

She hadn't heard him. But now she knew. In the morning, would he remember that he'd told her?

"Oh, God," she whispered, thinking that she was in more trouble than she'd even known.

As soon as she closed the door, Craig was in her head.

Thank God.

You were watching that.

Yeah.

You heard about...a murder.

Yeah.

What am I going to do?

Hope to hell he doesn't focus on it when he wakes up.

As she caught the raw edge in his silent voice, she shuddered. Then she picked up that he was thinking about her in bed with Reynard, not about the man's murderous past. He already knew about that.

But now the dark and dangerous images swirling in his mind made her gasp. *You can't break in here. Don't try. They'll catch you.*

I'm coming in for you.

Wait

I will. I'll figure something out.

She pulled off her gown and shoes and found a long T-shirt she could wear—something very unsexy, if John appeared in her room.

She knew Craig caught that thought and tried to ignore his instant flare of anger. But then she walked to the desk, picked up a letter opener she'd seen there and set it on the bedside table.

She heard Craig catch his breath.

You think you could get out of there alive if you stabbed him?

You have a better idea?

Wait for me to get there.

Praying that was possible, she washed her face, brushed her teeth and used the toilet before climbing into bed.

Closing her eyes, she imagined Craig lying beside her.

Soon, he whispered in her mind, and she hoped it was going to work out the way they wanted.

She made a strangled sound when she felt his lips against hers.

Her eyes flew open, but the room was empty.

How did you do that?

In the darkness she heard him chuckle.

It's like moving books in the bookcase. Only more fun. As she heard his voice in her mind, she felt his invisible fingers stroking her hair, her arms. When he cupped his palms around her breasts, she caught her breath.

What are you doing?

What we both want to do.

You shouldn't. When she tried to sit up, he pressed his hand against her shoulder. *Don't run away from me.*

But you're making me hot. And what can I do about it?

He laughed again. *I can do something about it. You've had a terrible day. Let me make it up to you.*

It's not your fault.

You begged me to take you with me. I wouldn't listen.

She swallowed hard. *But that might have gotten you killed. I think that blast at the cabin was meant for you.*

Yeah. And the poor cop was just at the wrong place at the wrong time. But let's not focus on that now.

As he spoke, he brushed his invisible lips against hers as he lifted and shaped her breasts. She closed her eyes, unable to pull away from the sensations. And as she enjoyed his kisses and his touch, it was difficult to remember that he wasn't there in the bed with her. When his thumbs and fingers closed around her nipples, she had to take her lower lip between her teeth to keep from crying out. That was all she needed—to bring someone charging down the hall. She didn't allow herself to actually name who that might be.

She squirmed against the mattress.

Stop.

You don't like it?

You know I do.

Than let me give you pleasure.

But...

He stopped her protest with a long, passionate kiss as he tugged at one nipple while his other hand drifted down her body toward the juncture of her legs.

She didn't have to open them for him. Using his phantom

hands, he had complete access to the most intimate parts of her, and she caught his satisfaction in knowing what he was doing to her.

Her hips rose and fell as he stroked a finger through her folds, dipping into her and turning his finger in a maddening circle, then traveling upward to the point of her greatest sensation. He kept up the arousing attentions, making it impossible for her to focus on anything else as he drove her up and up toward a climax that burst over and through her, making her gasp as she struggled not to cry out in pleasure.

And when he was finished, he whispered in her mind, *Sleep now. You need your rest.*

What about you? she managed to ask.

That was good for me, too. And it gives me something to look forward to. When I get you back, we'll finish what we started.

She prayed that he was right. Prayed that he would be able to get her away from the man who refused to allow her to escape from him.

STEPHANIE WOKE with the memory of making love with Craig and a smile on her face. She'd dreamed of having a relationship like that, but she'd been sure it would never happen for her, until she met Craig.

She whispered his name and turned her head, expecting to see him lying beside her. Then reality slammed back like a prison door clanging behind her.

She wasn't with Craig. Not at all. She was in a bedroom in John Reynard's house. Thank the Lord, not Reynard's bedroom.

She clenched her hands into fists, wanting to pound them against the walls for all the good that would do her.

When she glanced at the bedside table, she saw the letter opener she'd put there—which looked as if she'd been expecting to be attacked in the night.

Hoping that no one had checked in on her, she put the weapon back on the desk and went to the bathroom, where she got ready and pulled on jeans and a T-shirt.

People were moving around the house when she came down, and John and Claire were sitting at the dining-room table, talking as intimately as they had been in the lounge the night before.

As she watched them together, she wanted to ask why John just didn't marry Claire, since they were so obviously suited to each other, but she kept the question to herself.

"There she is," Claire said.

"Yes, we let you get your beauty sleep," John added as he gave her a considering look. "I'm sorry I drank so much last night. It won't happen again."

While she was scrambling for a reply, he said, "The wedding will be this afternoon."

"What?" she gasped, feeling as if the breath had been knocked out of her. "I thought you wanted a morning wedding."

"I changed my mind," he answered.

"Yes. We have almost everything arranged," Claire said brightly.

Unable to stand, Stephanie dropped into a chair at the table. She'd known that John wanted to move quickly, but she'd had no idea the wedding would be today,

Claire bustled over and set a notebook in front of her. "Since you were asleep, I took the liberty of making some selections. I thought Prestige would be an ideal caterer. They're bringing the food from their kitchen in New Orleans. But I know there's a branch of Just for You Flowers about twenty minutes away, so we can use them. I've sent out email invitations to a number of John's business associates, and I've already received some replies, but I think we can expect a small group—perhaps twenty guests. And we'll have your father picked up and brought here. We decided that a justice of the peace was the easiest choice for an official. Mr. Vincent Lacey will be here at five."

Stephanie fought a wave of dizziness. "Five? The ceremony is at five?"

"Yes. Your dress has also arrived. And I can do your hair and makeup. That's what I used to do—for one of the local TV stations before I came to work for you."

"Oh" was all Stephanie could say, ordering herself not to start shaking. She had to hold it together but knew she was on the edge of a meltdown. And the worst part was that when she tried to contact Craig, she couldn't locate him. He seemed to have fallen off the edge of the earth again.

HAROLD GODDARD ENDED the phone call with a broad grin on his face. He had some good news for a change. He'd known from his men that someone else was looking for Stephanie Swift and Craig Branson in Houma.

There was a chance it could be someone who knew about the clinic's purpose, but he doubted it. Maybe this had to do with her fiancé, John Reynard. Harold had used the old Reynard murder connection to get Craig and Stephanie together. But it looked as if Reynard wasn't prepared to give her up.

And now there was a massive mobilization at Reynard's country estate. Mobilization for a quickie wedding. Caterer, florist, a justice of the peace. The works.

Which made it pretty clear that Stephanie wasn't dead. Reynard must have taken her back to the plantation. Maybe his men had even blown up that cottage and killed Branson.

Now Reynard was going to make sure his bride didn't escape again. Harold tapped his finger against his lips, thinking. He'd sent two guys to Houma, but it looked as if Reynard had a lot more than that at the plantation. Harold had better get some extra help and send them down there.

The plantation was fenced in—with a gate. But the guards would be expecting wedding guests, which meant it wouldn't be that hard to crash the gate and snatch the bride.

Of course, Branson was out of the picture now, but it would be very instructive to see what had happened to Stephanie with her lover gone. He'd examine her mental state, then put her out of her misery.

CRAIG HAD BEEN BUSY. Last night he'd spent some time in the bathroom of the cheap motel where he was staying, using a clipper on his thick dark hair and then shaving his head. He'd cut himself a couple of times, but the effect of the hair removal was startling. He didn't recognize the ugly-looking man who stared back at him in the mirror. Hopefully, Reynard wouldn't, either.

Next he took a chance and wired five thousand dollars from an account he kept under another name to a Western Union office in a nearby town.

He'd used some of the cash to buy spy equipment to monitor phone communications at the plantation, and that had already paid off. Reynard was planning his wedding for that afternoon.

Craig swore. The bastard was moving fast. But as he listened to the preparations, he got an idea.

After learning Reynard's plans, he stopped at a discount department store and bought some extra shirts, which he put on in layers, bulking up his body to change his physique a little. As he passed the cosmetics department, he had another couple of ideas. He bought a dark eyebrow pencil and fake tanning cream. He spent some time in the men's room putting on the tanning stuff and doing his eyebrows, trying to make them look thicker but natural. Next he stopped in the hardware store and bought some little rubber rings, which he stuck into his nostrils to make his nose look bigger. After altering his appearance, he ran a couple more errands. With the state's lenient gun laws, he was also able to pick up a SIG semiautomatic with a couple of spare clips—plus some other equipment he was going to need.

When he was as prepared as he could be, he drove to Just for You Flowers, where the staff was frantically working to get the Reynard order ready in time.

He'd asked for a wedding bouquet of white roses and baby's breath plus several vases of flowers in stands to decorate the pool area where the wedding was being held.

"Hi, I'm Cal Barnes from the New Orleans store," he told the woman behind the counter. "When they heard you were doing a job for John Reynard, they sent me down here to help."

She gave him an annoyed look, and he was pretty sure that with his bald head and heavy eyebrows, he looked like a thug.

"No need. We have it under control," she said.

But I'm going to drive the van that brings in the flowers, Craig said, putting in every ounce of mental energy he could muster. He'd done this before with Sam. He'd done it with Stephanie. He'd never done it on his own, but he knew Stephanie had been pushing John in the direction she wanted, and if she could do it, so could he. He reinforced the silent observation with a second repetition.

The woman's expression was still doubtful. "I'm just going to call Phil at the New Orleans shop and check on that."

"It was Phil who sent me."

She reached for the phone, and he sent her a fast and

furious message. *Don't call Phil. Don't call Phil. You need Barnes to drive the truck.*

He kept repeating the message, waiting with his heart pounding. If she didn't take him up on the offer, he'd have to go to plan B, and he had no freaking idea what that was. But he *had* to get inside that plantation compound, if he had a chance of rescuing Stephanie before she ended up in Reynard's bed tonight.

"We could use a driver. Some of the stands we'll need are heavy, and we only have women in the shop today."

"I'm glad to help with that," Craig said.

"And while you're here, there are some deliveries that need to be put in the refrigerator."

SEVERAL MILES AWAY, Rachel and Jake Harper were tuned in to the preparations at the estate.

"He's going to marry her this afternoon," Rachel said, a note of disgust in her voice. "And Craig Branson is ready to go in there and rescue her."

"He could get himself killed," her husband answered.

"I know that. And I want this to come out okay for them. What can we do about it?"

"I should say—nothing," Jake answered firmly.

She gave him an incredulous look. "You'd leave two of the children from the Solomon Clinic in terrible danger?"

"I didn't say I'd do that, but we have to think carefully about what we're risking."

"I know. But maybe we'd better start making some contingency plans."

He answered with a tight nod, and she knew he would go along with her plans—if he didn't think they were too dangerous.

She also knew he had grown up on the streets, committed to no one but himself. Caring about no one but himself.

He'd bonded with her because of the telepathic link they'd forged, but it was still difficult for him to see the importance of extending that bond to the others. Especially after the first children from the clinic that they'd met had started off by attacking them.

Chapter Eighteen

Trying to act as if his brain wasn't going to explode from tension, Craig went to work helping unload roses and gladioli. Then he tried to look busy while he watched the woman who was putting together bouquets, hoping he could do a credible job of flower arranging. It looked like the trick to making them stay in place was anchoring the stems in some kind of rigid foam stuff.

And all the time he kept projecting the message that nobody had to check up on him at the New Orleans office. He was supposed to be at the local shop. He couldn't be sure if it would work, and he kept thinking that if it didn't, he might have to pull a gun and herd the two women into the refrigerator, while he stole the van and went to the wedding.

Every minute that ticked by made him feel a little closer to pulling off the delivery scheme. But that didn't stop his mind from churning, because there was no way to know if his plan would work until after he got into the estate. More than that, he knew Stephanie had to be sick with worry about the upcoming wedding, but there was too much activity around the plantation for him to risk going until closer to the big event. The best he could do was to keep sending messages, telling her he was coming. Telling her it was all going to turn out okay, even when he was pretty sure she couldn't hear him.

Unfortunately, he wasn't picking up anything from her, and that had him worried, even though he kept telling himself they were simply too far apart.

STEPHANIE'S CHEST was so tight that she could barely breathe. While she ate breakfast, she covertly watched John. But he gave no sign that he remembered anything from the evening before.

Of course, that could all be an act. One of his main goals was to never have anyone think less of him. Even her and Claire, so he put up a good front.

After she'd done her best to pretend that she was hungry, he pushed back his chair and stood up.

"I should leave you ladies to the preparations," he said, his voice casual, though she knew he was hiding his own tension.

"We'll be ready for you at five," Claire said in a chipper voice.

Right, Stephanie thought. *Why don't you just stand in for me, since you're apparently enjoying sleeping with him?*

"I'll be in my office if you need anything," he added.

Stephanie nodded.

As soon as he was out of the room, she felt marginally better.

"You have nothing to worry about," Claire said.

"Mmm-hmm," she answered, wanting to scream at the woman who had been betraying her all along.

"Do you know how lucky you are?" Claire asked.

"Yes," she said. She was thinking she was so lucky to have met Craig, and he was going to get her out of this.

Or die trying? That stray thought had her insides going cold. She knew he was going to try to get in here, but she didn't know how.

"You should start with a nice relaxing bath," Claire said.

"I'm thinking about what order we should do stuff in. First the bath. Then we can do your finger- and toenails. Then your hair and makeup. What color do you want for your nails?"

From the sideboard she brought over a box of nail-polish bottles. "I think a pale pink would look good with your coloring."

Stephanie agreed because she had no interest in the color. Or maybe bloodred would be best. Then it wouldn't show on her hands if she ended up in bed with John and scratched her nails down his face.

She canceled that thought as soon as it surfaced, knowing it was dangerous to give Claire even a hint of her real feelings.

Instead she said, "Yes, let's go with pink." At least getting herself all prettied up would give her something to do until the hateful ceremony.

And then what? She kept thinking of something she'd heard about the 1950s. Back then, the Soviet Union had been the major threat to America, and people had debated "Better dead than red or better red than dead?"

In other words, if you succumbed to the enemy, could you bide your time and hope to free yourself?

She knew that was true for the countries that had been Soviet satellites. They'd stuck it out and come through the dark period. And many of them now had democratically elected governments.

All of that was well and good in theory. But could she stand to go to bed with John Reynard? Stand to have him kiss her, touch her? Be inside her? And what else would he want her to do to him?

When she couldn't stop herself from shuddering, Claire touched her arm. "I know you've been through a terrible experience," she murmured. "Maybe it would help to tell me about it."

So you can report to John, Stephanie thought, but she only shook her head. "I don't want to dwell on it."

"I understand."

Yeah, I'll bet you do, she thought with a note of sarcasm. Aloud she said, "I'd like to take that bath now."

If they had to have a wedding night, maybe she could get him drunk again. Or would that work twice in a row? And she couldn't do it every night of her life. Eventually…

She cut off that thought, because she couldn't let it come to that.

HAROLD GODDARD WAITED impatiently to hear from the men he was sending into the Reynard compound.

When Wayne finally called, he snatched up the phone. "What?"

"There's a lot of activity at the estate. Delivery trucks going into the compound. Two catering trucks."

"And anyone going in and out is getting stopped at the main gate?"

"Yeah."

Harold thought for a moment. Were they really expecting an attack, or was Reynard just taking precautions because that was his M.O.? Finally he said, "I think he's not really expecting trouble. I mean, who would go up against him? I've hacked his email. The wedding ceremony's at five. Wait till then, then crash the gate. You'll know where the woman is, and you can take her and run."

"What about collateral damage?"

"Do what you have to."

Chapter Nineteen

The flower delivery was scheduled for three-thirty in the afternoon. Craig's tension mounted as the departure time approached. And he breathed out a sigh when he finally drove away from the loading dock in back of the flower shop. He made one more stop, at a spot where he'd left the extra equipment he was going to need, packing it into the back of the panel truck behind the flowers.

He said a silent prayer that he wasn't going to get Stephanie killed, then headed for the main gate of Reynard's estate and waited with his heart pounding while he sized up the operation. At the gate there were three guards. One of them asked for his credentials and checked them over carefully, as if the president of a foreign country was staying here and needed special protection.

"I'd like a look in that truck," the man said.

"Sure," Craig agreed as though he didn't have a thing in the world to hide. Like, for example, that he was here to kidnap the bride. Climbing out, he walked around to the back and opened the door.

There's nothing in here but flowers. All you see is flowers, Craig said over and over as the guy climbed inside and poked around.

Flowers. Just flowers. And I'm just the delivery guy, doing his job.

The guard jumped out. "You're good to go," he said.

"Thanks." He waited a beat.

"Yes?"

"Where should I park?"

"Around the side of the house. The ceremony is out by the pool."

"Okay. Thanks."

He would have liked to ask more questions about the layout of the estate, but he assumed he was supposed to know. He still wasn't sure what "around the side of the house" meant, but when he spotted a catering truck pulled up near the triple garage, he breathed out a little sigh. Before parking, he turned around so that he was facing outward, poised for a quick getaway. But he figured that would look normal because he was unloading the flowers from the back.

After climbing out, he followed one of the catering guys to the back of the house. Chairs had been set up on either side of an aisle, facing a bank of bushes. Over to the side were six round tables, with snowy-white cloths where china and cutlery had already been set out.

He tried to remember what he knew about wedding ceremonies, which wasn't much. Probably they wanted a big bouquet of flowers on either side of the open space in front of the bushes, because presumably that was where the ceremony was being held.

Someone came hurrying out of the house. He turned, hoping against hope to see Stephanie.

Instead it was a dark-haired woman that he recognized immediately. She was Stephanie's assistant, the one he'd met at the dress shop a lifetime ago.

He forced himself to stand in a relaxed posture with his hands at his sides as she gave him a long look. As he faced her, he furiously sent her the message. *You do not know me. You never saw me before in your life.*

She tipped her head to the side. "Do I know you?"

He kept projecting the silent message as he lowered his voice an octave. "No. Are you the bride?"

She laughed. "No, I'm Mr. Reynard's assistant."

Mr. Reynard's assistant. Last time he'd seen her, she'd been Stephanie's assistant. It seemed she'd come up in the world, or maybe she'd been working for Reynard all along.

"Let me give you the bride's bouquet," he said, leading her back to where he'd left the van. "And then you can show me where you want the flowers placed."

"You do have the centerpieces, right?"

"Of course," he answered quickly. Yeah, there would be flowers on the tables.

He led her to where he'd parked the van, then opened the back door and got out the box with the flowers the bride was to carry, feeling a pang as he handed them to her. A wedding bouquet for the woman he loved, only it wasn't *their* wedding.

She gave the flowers a brief inspection. "Very nice."

"Thank you," he answered, thinking, from her expression and the tone of her voice, that she wished they were hers. Too bad Reynard couldn't have picked a bride who wanted to marry him, but probably he was too obsessed with the prestige of marrying into an old New Orleans family, and with thinking Stephanie had heard him discussing murder.

As soon as she took the flowers away, he dragged in a breath and let it out. This might be the best time to contact Stephanie. She'd be alone. At least, he didn't think Reynard would be with her.

He sent his mind out to her. *Stephanie.*

He felt her jolt of recognition when she heard him.

Craig?

Yes.

Thank God. Oh, thank God.

I just saw Claire. She came down to get the flowers.

Yes, she was apparently working for John all along.

I think she's on her way back to you—with your bouquet. But I have to tell you some stuff while we have a chance. I'm the guy delivering the flowers.

Apparently his previous words had registered.

Did you say she saw you?

Yes, but she didn't recognize me. I have on a few shirts to bulk me up. And I'm the bald guy with the splotchy tan and the dark eyebrows.

She caught her breath.

Yeah, I look like hell, but so far the disguise is working.

What are we going to do?

You've been manipulating his mind, right?

Yes. Like when I got him drunk last night so he couldn't... Her silent voice trailed off.

We're going to do it again. And I've got something else planned.

When he told her what he'd brought with him, she sucked in a sharp breath. *Claire's back.*

I'll see you in a little while.

Light classical music had begun to play as he carried the large vases of flowers to the spot where the bride and groom would stand and fluffed up the arrangements, then began taking the smaller arrangements to the tables, setting one in the center of each. The effect was quite nice. Too bad it was going to be screwed up when the guests stampeded.

And here they were. As he worked, he saw well-dressed men and women arriving and gathering in an area at the side of the pool where a bar had been set up. One of them was Stephanie's father, who was holding a glass of clear liquid.

Water? He remembered that the old guy drank too much. Maybe he was trying to be on his best behavior today.

Craig saw Reynard at the edge of the crowd and sent him a message. *Go get yourself a nice big drink.*

He was elated when the man approached the bar and got a glass of whiskey. But instead of drinking, he looked at it for a long moment and left it on the bar.

Craig felt his stomach muscles tighten. Apparently Reynard didn't want to repeat last night's nonperformance.

He was focused on Reynard and his guests when he felt a tingling at the back of his neck.

Turning, he saw one of Reynard's guards stoop to pick up the knapsack he'd left at the edge of the patio. When the man started to open it, Craig strode over.

"That's mine," he said aloud. Silently he added, *There's nothing you have to worry about in there.*

"What's in it?"

"I'm from the florist. That's extra stuff I might need." *Nothing to worry about.*

"I'll just take a look."

Too bad the mental push wasn't working on this guy.

"We should step around the corner so we don't disturb the guests," Craig said.

The man looked toward the crowd at the bar where Reynard was chatting to a group of men and women. "Yeah."

They rounded the corner of the house.

When the guy bent to look inside the knapsack, Craig chopped him on the back of the neck, and he went down. But now what?

He pulled the guy into the bushes and opened the knapsack, where he'd stowed some duct tape. He used it to tape the guy's mouth and secure his hands and feet. Then he hit him on the back of the head with the butt of the SIG, hoping that would keep him quiet.

His heart was thumping inside his chest as he rushed back to the pool area.

Men in uniform moved through the crowd, apparently telling the guests to take their seats because they began to find chairs.

When everyone was seated, a rotund gray-haired man clad in black walked to the front area and stood between the tall vases Craig had placed there.

Then the music switched to the traditional wedding march.

As all eyes turned to the patio door, Craig's breath caught. Stephanie was standing just inside the entrance in a long white dress, gripping her father's arm. She looked achingly beautiful, and also pale and breathless. Her father looked like a cat that had finished a saucer of cream.

From the corner of his eye, Craig saw Reynard take his place at the front of the assembly and look back toward his bride, his expression a mixture of relief and satisfaction.

Stephanie and her father were about halfway down the aisle when one of Reynard's guards came running toward his boss. He shouted, "Intruder alert. Intruder alert."

Reynard looked up as the man scanned the crowd, then pointed to Craig. Oh, Lord, maybe they'd caught the incident with the other guy and the knapsack on a security camera.

It wasn't time for the diversion he'd planned, but he had no choice now.

Reaching into his knapsack, he pulled out some of the fireworks he'd bought in town, touched a lighter to the fuse of one and tossed it beside the pool. He did the same with several more.

They began shooting off sparks and smoke, sending panicked screams through the crowd as they mowed down chairs in their haste to get to safety.

Craig could hear chairs crashing to the ground. One of

the fleeing guests bumped into a table and tipped it over. And at least one splashed into the pool.

As he'd planned, people were creating chaos as they tried to get away before they got burned.

Over here. I'm over here, Craig shouted in his mind. There was as much smoke as sparks now, and it was hard to see, but he also knew that he could bring Stephanie toward him by using their mind-to-mind contact.

He drew his gun, hoping he didn't have to start shooting, because innocent bystanders would get hurt.

To his relief, Stephanie came stumbling out of the smoke, and she was also holding a pistol.

Where did you get that?

I asked one of the guards, and he gave it to me—to protect myself.

Stupid of him, given the circumstances. But then, Reynard still thinks I'm dead.

As he spoke, he was leading her around the pool toward the side of the house where he'd left the van.

He ached to pull her into his arms, but there was no time for that.

This way.

He directed her toward the waiting delivery van, praying that they could get out before Reynard realized where they'd gone.

Stephanie jumped into the passenger seat, and he saw her clawing at the white dress. She tore a rip down the front and wiggled out, throwing the dress into the back of the van. Underneath she was wearing a pair of shorts and a halter top.

He had started the engine and was headed for the gate when a group of men came running out of the woods, shooting at the van.

Lord, who were they? Not Reynard's security men.

Stephanie gasped.

I see one of the men who kidnapped us, Stephanie shouted in his mind. *They're here, and there are more guys with them.*

He tried to cope with that, tried to reason how they had gotten here. They must still be after Stephanie, and they must have seen him lead her toward the van.

The invasion force ran toward the van shooting, and behind the vehicle, Reynard's men were also charging forward and also shooting, and Reynard was with them, firing along with the rest.

"Duck down," Craig shouted as he plowed forward, turning left and driving in a zigzag pattern, hoping he could keep himself and Stephanie alive long enough to escape.

Intruder alert. Intruder alert, Stephanie shouted beside him. *Shoot at the invaders. Shoot at the invaders, not the van.*

He took up the chant, adding his voice to hers. Some of Reynard's men got the message and began firing at the men who had poured onto the property. The newcomers returned fire. But others kept aiming at the van.

And then another voice, louder and stronger, added force to the order.

Shoot at each other, not the van.

Who's that? Stephanie asked.

No idea. Could it be the woman who put us in communication?

Maybe.

For a heart-stopping moment, nothing seemed to change. Then Reynard's men began blasting in earnest at the others, and the invaders blasted back.

Craig looked behind them and saw Reynard still coming, determined not to let his bride escape.

He knew Stephanie caught the thought because she gasped as she followed his line of sight.

Craig kept aiming for the gate. And for long moments he thought they would get away. Then, to his horror, the van began to sputter, and he knew the engine had been hit. Finally it coughed and stopped.

Chapter Twenty

"We have to make a run for it, but wait until I throw more fireworks," Craig shouted, opening the driver's door and ducking behind it as he set off two more cones and lobbed them behind him.

Reynard leaped out of the smoke, murder in his eyes as he raised his gun at Craig.

Before he could fire, Craig heard the crack of a pistol.

Reynard's eyes took on a look of shock as he went down. When Craig turned his head, he saw Stephanie had shot the man.

She gasped as she stared at her former fiancé.

"I had to do it."

"Thanks for saving my life."

They both crouched low, running forward as the gun battle raged behind them, but there was still a guard at the gate.

"Halt or I'll shoot."

"I'm trying to get Miss Stephanie out of the line of fire," Craig shouted back.

"The hell you are." He gestured toward the uproar in back of them. "I think you caused whatever's going on back there."

"No," Craig denied, but the man advanced on them, gun drawn.

"Drop your weapons."

With no choice, Craig and Stephanie dropped their guns. They had gotten this far, but they were still inside the compound.

The man held the pistol on them, using his walkie-talkie to call the other stations.

"What's going on back there?" he asked.

Static crackled on the line.

"Intruder came in to kidnap the bride. Fox is down. Repeat, Fox is down."

Fox must be the code name for Reynard, Craig thought.

Be ready to drop, he said to Stephanie. He knew she had picked up on what he was doing and was getting ready to send him power, but she stayed on her feet.

Craig had dropped his gun, but he still had the lighter in his hand. While the guard was distracted by the walkie-talkie message, Craig flicked the lighter on, using his mind to shoot out a tongue of flame toward the guard. When the man screamed and jumped back, Craig ducked low and rushed him, plowing his head into the guy's middle and bringing him down.

As they grappled for the weapon, Stephanie rushed in and kicked the guy in the head, stunning him.

Craig grabbed the gun and slammed it into the guard's face. As he and Stephanie started for the gate, he saw two figures had emerged from the wood, a man and a woman, advancing slowly.

Hurry, the woman shouted inside his head.

He and Stephanie picked up speed, but he heard running feet behind them. Guards who had escaped the gun battle were closing in.

As they pelted toward freedom, a bullet whizzed past his head, apparently shot from too far away for accuracy.

The woman raised her hand, lightning crackling at her fingertips. She sent it flying toward the cameras at the guard post. They sizzled and exploded, hopefully wiping out a visual of what had happened at the gate.

Power, give me power, the woman shouted inside his head.

Craig wasn't sure what he was doing, but both he and Stephanie tried their best to send her additional energy, just as they had done with each other.

When he heard roaring, crackling noises, he turned his head and saw a wall of flame erupt, creating a barrier between them and the advancing guards.

Shouts of fear and curses of anger reached him, but none of the bullets were getting through.

You can't keep that up forever. Let's get the hell out of here. This time it was the man speaking.

As the fire burned behind them, the man grabbed the woman's arm and pulled her away. Craig and Stephanie followed.

The four of them raced into the woods, then into a clearing where a four-wheel-drive SUV sat. The man and woman climbed in front, with the man behind the wheel. Craig and Stephanie climbed in the back.

Before they'd clicked their seat belts, he took off, jouncing along a dirt road. The ride smoothed out as they came out onto a two-lane highway.

In the backseat, Craig pulled Stephanie close and slung his arm around her shoulder, still trying to process everything that had happened.

"You're like us," he breathed, speaking to the people in the front seat.

"Yeah," the man answered.

"Thanks for showing up."

"We couldn't leave you in danger," the woman said as she turned around. "We haven't officially met. I'm Rachel Harper, and this is my husband, Jake."

"Again, thanks," Stephanie said.

"Who was after you?" Rachel asked. "I mean besides John Reynard's men."

"I don't know, exactly," Craig said. "But I think it had something to do with the Solomon Clinic, since they apparently knew to show up in Houma."

Jake Harper cursed and glanced at his wife. "I thought we were done with that."

"Why?" Stephanie asked.

"Dr. Solomon is dead. And so is Bill Wellington, who funded the project through a Washington think tank. That should have laid the past to rest. But it appears that someone is still hunting us."

"It looks like it," she murmured.

"Why are they doing it? What do they want?" Stephanie asked.

"The Howell Institute fronted the money for a lot of pie-in-the-sky projects for the Defense Department and other agencies. Solomon convinced them he could create superintelligent children by manipulating fertilized eggs."

"So his clinic was a source of the eggs."

"Exactly. And when the kids turned out to have normal intelligence, Wellington shut the project down."

"Why isn't that the end of it?"

"Because of what we are," Jake answered. "We've got powers they don't understand. Which makes us a threat, or maybe an asset that someone can exploit."

Stephanie shuddered.

"One good thing about the situation—whoever was stalking you sent an invasion force to the wedding."

"Why is that good?" Craig asked.

"Because they took out a lot of the guards, and the guests saw the battle. They know the invaders are responsible for anything bad that happened."

"Like Reynard's death," Stephanie murmured.

"Exactly," Craig said.

"But that's the only upside. Until we figure out who is after us this time, I think it's best if you stay at the Lafayette plantation."

"You have a plantation?" Stephanie asked.

"It actually belongs to Gabriella Bordeaux. She and Luke Buckley are also products of the clinic. They were on the run, too. And hooked up with us."

As they drove west, Stephanie slumped against Craig.

We don't know what happened back at Reynard's estate. I don't even know if my father is all right.

He is. I saw him duck under a table.

Well, he got what he wanted. Reynard paid his debts, and I didn't have to marry the man.

She let her head drop to Craig's shoulder, and he held her close, marveling that she was in his arms and the two of them were finally safe.

Rachel broke into their silent conversation.

"The plantation's a good place for you to hide out—until we get the mess straightened out."

"You think we can?"

"Yes," she answered with conviction. "And I hope you want to join us in our group defense efforts."

"Of course," Craig said. "What you did back there was pretty impressive. How did you do that trick with the lightning bolt?"

"It's not difficult. We can teach you." She huffed out a breath. "I'm sorry we didn't come to help you sooner, but we had to be sure about you."

"About our being children from the clinic?"

In the driver's seat, Jake made a wry sound. "No. That part was pretty obvious. She means sure that you were friendly. The first people we met from the clinic tried to kill us."

Stephanie gasped. "Why?"

"They thought they were the only ones with our kind of mental powers, and they couldn't stand the idea of anyone else having them."

"Nice," Craig answered.

"You were a twin?" Rachel asked Craig.

"Yes. My brother, Sam, and I must have developed powers together right from the beginning. When he was killed, I thought I'd never find that again." He pulled Stephanie closer as he spoke. "Then I found Stephanie and discovered there was more than what Sam and I had shared."

As they drove to Lafayette, Jake and Rachel told them about the plantation. And they spoke about the clinic.

"Right now, the two of you probably want to decompress," Jake said.

"There are guest cottages on the grounds," Rachel said. "You can have one."

Craig was still feeling dazed as they pulled onto the Lafayette plantation property. He blinked when he saw the sign for Chez Gabriella.

"She was a pastry chef in New Orleans," Jake explained. "She's funding the plantation with this restaurant in the main house—where she grew up. But it's only open on the weekends. That gives us the run of the place the rest of the time. We're going to move the housing farther from the restaurant, but we haven't gotten around to it."

When he pulled up in front of a semicircle of cottages, another man and woman came walking down from the main house.

"Gabriella and Luke," Jake said.

They climbed out, and the newcomers hurried forward.

Jake made the introductions.

"It's so great to meet you. We wanted to come along, but Jake said we needed to stay here," Gabriella said.

They all shook hands, and Craig cleared his throat. "Try to imagine me with hair. I shaved my head for a disguise."

"We'll wait for the real you to emerge," Stephanie said. "Trust me, he's a handsome guy. And twenty pounds lighter than he looks."

"There's so much to tell you," Gabriella said, "but I know the two of you want some alone time."

"The restaurant's closed today, but I'm cooking for us. Come over around seven and we'll all have dinner."

"Thank you so much," Craig answered.

Gabriella showed them to one of the cottages. They stepped inside, and Craig had only a vague impression of antique furnishings because he was too focused on Stephanie to notice anything else. He reached for her and folded her into his arms. They hugged each other fiercely, both of them hardly able to believe that they'd escaped from Reynard's compound.

"Thank God you got there," Stephanie murmured.

"Thank God you kept your head and helped me."

He cut off the conversation by lowering his mouth to hers for a kiss that spoke of all the powerful emotions surging through him.

You were alone for so long. You never have to be again. I have you.

And you showed me what it is to have a partner who is everything two people can be to each other—and more.

It's just sinking in how much danger you put yourself in—for me.

For us.

I had to. You know I had to. And it worked out.

When they finally came up for air, she ran her hands up and down his arms, over his back, and he knew she was reassuring herself by the contact with his strong body.

"This place must have a bedroom."

"I hope so."

Linking his hand with hers, he led her into the next room and stepped far enough away to look at her outfit.

"How could you put on a halter top and shorts under your wedding gown?"

She laughed. "I did it while Claire was out of the room. I knew I couldn't run very far in that gown."

"You looked so beautiful, and then you ripped the dress apart."

"We'll get another one—for us."

He laughed. "Is that a proposal?"

When she flushed, he kissed her. *I'm just teasing. You know I want the same thing you do.*

He untied the halter. *Convenient. No bra.*

His eyes were warm as he looked at her.

She reached for the buttons of his shirt, then found another layer underneath—and another. "Not so convenient."

He helped her unbutton the shirts and shrugged out of them.

She ran her hand across his broad chest, winnowing her fingers through the crinkly hair she found there.

He sighed and pulled her close, swaying her breasts against his chest.

His mouth came back to her, his tongue playing with the seam of her lips. She opened for him, closing her eyes as he deepened the kiss while he cupped her breasts in his hands and slid his thumbs over the taut peaks, wringing a glad cry from her.

JOY SURGED THROUGH STEPHANIE. She was free to be with Craig now, and that thought sent hot, needy sensations curling through her body.

He unbuttoned her shorts and lowered the zipper, pushing the garment down her legs, along with her panties, so he could touch her intimately, sending heat pounding through her.

He had brought her to climax the night before. Now she needed more. And she needed to return the pleasure he had given her.

She pulled back the covers, bringing him down to the surface of the bed with her, clasping him to her before rising up and trailing kisses along his body, moving ever downward, knowing he was tensing with anticipation. And when she found his erection with her mouth and closed around him, she felt his pleasure zinging through her.

He didn't have to tell her when to stop. She knew. And she knew when to straddle his body and bring him inside her.

She was dizzy with desire. And she knew he was, too.

She had kept things slow. Now an explosion of need had her moving in a frantic rhythm that sent them both flying off into space.

When she came down to earth, he was there to catch her.

Emotions flooded through her as they looked at each other.

"This is so much more than I ever expected from my life. Oh, Craig, I love you so much."

"I love you. And I'm going to make sure nobody can snatch you away from me."

"You think we're still in danger?" she breathed.

"I think we have to stay hidden until we find out who was after us." He dragged in a breath and let it out. "I came to New Orleans to punish my brother's killer, because I thought that satisfaction was all I could expect. Then I met you, and I knew that there was so much more."

"Never alone again," she whispered as she snuggled against him, marveling at what she had found with this man. Now and for the rest of her life.

* * * * *

REQUEST YOUR FREE BOOKS!
2 FREE NOVELS PLUS 2 FREE GIFTS!

❤ HARLEQUIN®

INTRIGUE®

BREATHTAKING ROMANTIC SUSPENSE

YES! Please send me 2 FREE Harlequin Intrigue® novels and my 2 FREE gifts (gifts are worth about $10). After receiving them, if I don't wish to receive any more books, I can return the shipping statement marked "cancel." If I don't cancel, I will receive 6 brand-new novels every month and be billed just $4.74 per book in the U.S. or $5.24 per book in Canada. That's a savings of at least 14% off the cover price! It's quite a bargain! Shipping and handling is just 50¢ per book in the U.S. and 75¢ per book in Canada.* I understand that accepting the 2 free books and gifts places me under no obligation to buy anything. I can always return a shipment and cancel at any time. Even if I never buy another book, the two free books and gifts are mine to keep forever.

182/382 HDN F43C

Name _____ (PLEASE PRINT) _____

Address _____ Apt. # _____

City _____ State/Prov. _____ Zip/Postal Code _____

Signature (if under 18, a parent or guardian must sign)

Mail to the **Harlequin® Reader Service:**
IN U.S.A.: P.O. Box 1867, Buffalo, NY 14240-1867
IN CANADA: P.O. Box 609, Fort Erie, Ontario L2A 5X3

**Are you a subscriber to Harlequin Intrigue books
and want to receive the larger-print edition?
Call 1-800-873-8635 or visit www.ReaderService.com.**

* Terms and prices subject to change without notice. Prices do not include applicable taxes. Sales tax applicable in N.Y. Canadian residents will be charged applicable taxes. Offer not valid in Quebec. This offer is limited to one order per household. Not valid for current subscribers to Harlequin Intrigue books. All orders subject to credit approval. Credit or debit balances in a customer's account(s) may be offset by any other outstanding balance owed by or to the customer. Please allow 4 to 6 weeks for delivery. Offer available while quantities last.

Your Privacy—The Harlequin® Reader Service is committed to protecting your privacy. Our Privacy Policy is available online at www.ReaderService.com or upon request from the Harlequin Reader Service.

We make a portion of our mailing list available to reputable third parties that offer products we believe may interest you. If you prefer that we not exchange your name with third parties, or if you wish to clarify or modify your communication preferences, please visit us at www.ReaderService.com/consumerchoice or write to us at Harlequin Reader Service Preference Service, P.O. Box 9062, Buffalo, NY 14269. Include your complete name and address.

HIDIR13R

It was well after nine when Dalton finally called Briar to tell her he was coming up the front walkway. She hurried to unlock the door and let him in. "All stitched up?"

He nodded. "Want to see my wound?"

Smiling, she shook her head. "You hungry? Logan and I had chicken soup for dinner. I can heat some up for you."

He caught her hand as she moved toward the kitchen, his fingers warm and firm around hers. "Doyle and I grabbed a burger on the way home."

"How'd that go?" She waited for him to let go of her hand, but he twined his fingers with hers instead, leading her over to the sofa. He sat heavily, tugging her down beside him.

"It went…better than I expected. He wasn't a complete smart-ass, and I tried not to be a defensive jerk. So…progress." He gave her hands a light squeeze. "Logan asleep?"

She looked down at their twined hands, her gaze drawn by the intersection of her fair skin and his tanned fingers. "About thirty minutes ago. We had to read a couple of extra stories, and he was worried that you weren't home yet, but I explained you had to go somewhere with your brother. I also promised you'd look in on him before you go to bed. You don't have to, though. Once he falls asleep, it takes a bulldozer to wake him. He wouldn't know you were there."

"I'll know," he said, rolling his head toward her.

She met his gaze, a ripple of pure feminine awareness rolling through her, setting off a dozen tingles along her spine.

But was she woman enough to deal with a man like Dalton? A man who'd lived a life of privilege she couldn't even begin to imagine, much less understand? A man with his own demons that made her day-to-day struggles seem like bumps in the road in comparison?

"Last night," he murmured, "I wanted to kiss you."

She closed her eyes, overwhelmed by his raw honesty. "I know."

"I still do."

Can Briar and Dalton escape the clutches of an elusive enemy and have the happy future they both crave? Find out in THE LEGEND OF SMUGGLER'S CAVE by award-winning author Paula Graves, available April 2014 wherever Harlequin® Intrigue® books and ebooks are sold.

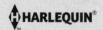
HARLEQUIN®

INTRIGUE®

USA TODAY **BESTSELLING AUTHOR
DELORES FOSSEN RETURNS TO
SILVER CREEK WITH THE SCORCHING
STORY OF A TEXAS LAWMAN WHO'LL
RISK EVERYTHING TO SAVE HIS
EX-LOVE—AND HIS UNBORN CHILD...**

FBI agent turned Texas deputy Josh Ryland is stunned to find pregnant hostages on a routine check for suspicious activity at a remote ranch. Even more shocking is the identity of one of the captives. Five months ago, Josh and FBI special agent Jaycee Finney shared a weekend of passion that ended badly. Now she's in danger—and claims he's her baby's father.

Jaycee owes Josh the truth. After her unwitting reckless behavior almost got him killed, the cowboy cop has good reason not to trust her. But with the ruthless mastermind of a black market baby ring gunning for her, it's Jaycee who has to trust Josh with her life…and the life of their child.

JOSH
BY DELORES FOSSEN

Available April 2014, only from Harlequin® Intrigue®.

HI69752

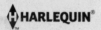
INTRIGUE®

THE ELITE CORCORAN TEAM HAS A NEW HERO IN HELENKAY DIMON'S *RELENTLESS!*

Branded a traitor for exposing high-level corruption, former NCIS agent Ben Tanner needs to redeem himself. When the hot new operative saves nurse Jocelyn Raine from a brutal attacker, he embarks on his most challenging mission yet: discovering who's after the strong, sexy woman— and trying his best not to fall for her. She has, he learns, something in her past that she wants to remain hidden.

But when the attacks on Jocelyn continue, Ben takes her on the run to protect her. Sparks ignite and tension is high as their options dwindle. It's possible Jocelyn's secret has endangered them both. Now it's Ben's job to see they survive the fallout….

RELENTLESS
BY HELENKAY DIMON

Available April 2014, only from Harlequin® Intrigue®.